"I want to take you to bed," he breathed

And Lyall grinned as his hands fastened on her arms. Through her sweater, Morgana was conscious of the pressure of his fingers, his touch burning her as if his hands lay on her bare flesh.

She faced him defiantly. "Let go of me, please."

"When I'm good and ready." Lyall's reply was curt. "You're a delectable little autocrat, but I give the orders here now."

"Not to me," she denied. "Never to me. Now take your hands off me."

His mouth twisted as he stared down at her. "You sound almost convincing. That outraged note is quite effective," he remarked. "The trouble is that I don't want to stop touching you, and if you're honest, you'll admit that isn't what you actually want, either."

SARA CRAVEN
is also the author of these

Harlequin Presents

and this

Harlequin Romance

SARA CRAVEN

witching hour

Harlequin Books

TORONTO • LONDON • LOS ANGELES • AMSTERDAM
SYDNEY • HAMBURG • PARIS • STOCKHOLM • ATHENS • TOKYO

Harlequin Presents edition published October 1981
ISBN 0-373-10459-6

Original hardcover edition published in 1981
by Mills & Boon Limited

CHAPTER ONE

THE October afternoon was fading fast, and the drawing room at Polzion House was filled with shadows, but in spite of the encroaching dimness, none of the lamps had been lit, and the log fire on the wide hearth had been allowed to burn away almost to ash.

In her grey dress with its long sleeves and high collar, Morgana seemed part of the shadows as she stood at the window, staring out at the wind-tossed garden. She was motionless, only her hands balled into fists at her sides giving any indication of the inner tension which threatened to consume her.

Outside the wind was rising. She could hear it wailing among the tall chimneys and along the eaves. Living on an exposed stretch of Cornish coastline, she had always taken autumn gales for granted, but today—the desolate sound of it made her shiver. On other, happier October afternoons, she would have drawn the curtains and turned to make up the fire, dismissing with a shrug whatever dark angel stood at her shoulder, but not now—perhaps not ever again. Not in this room—this house.

Something inside her cringed away from the thought, but it had to be faced. Her life at Polzion House, the only life she had ever known, would soon be at an end, and she had no idea, not even the slightest, what she could put in its place. It wasn't as if she was really trained for anything. Since leaving school with perfectly respectable examination results, she'd been here, helping her father and mother run the hotel. Family help had always been essential, as she'd always known, because Polzion House had never been successful or profitable enough to justify employing outside staff, with the exception of Elsa, who cooked like an angel when the fates decreed, and had been part of their lives for so long that she seemed like one of the family.

It had always been a struggle, but Morgana was young

5

and strong, and she had always been optimistic about the future, until now. Or until the day nearly a month ago when her whole world had fallen apart.

She swallowed with the pain of remembering thick in her throat. Her father hadn't been well for about a week, complaining almost apologetically of indigestion, and it was true Elsa's cooking had been more erratic than usual. So Morgana had not worried particularly. Her father was young for his age. He swam regularly, and played golf and squash. He was as fit as anyone could be, or so they had always thought, so his collapse when it came was doubly shocking.

She and her mother had lived in hope for about a week, visiting the hospital where he was in intensive care, telling each other that these days heart attacks were not serious—almost fashionable, in fact—and that all sorts of things could be done. But in Martin Pentreath's case, there was very little to be done. Years of strain and financial worry had taken their toll, and very quietly, they took him.

The funeral had been anguish. Everyone in the neighbourhood had been there to pay their last respects. Martin Pentreath had not been much of a hotelier, and even less of a business man, but everyone had liked him. Morgana had listened to their condolences, and told herself if she could get through this without breaking down, then everything would be all right. Only it had not been all right.

For Elizabeth Pentreath and her daughter there were shocks and more anguish when it came to the reading of the will, with Mr Trevick's solemn face even more portentous than usual. And Morgana, listening dazedly to words like 'entail' and 'surviving male heir', realised for the first time that with her father's death the life she had known and the future she expected had died too.

The door behind her opened suddenly, flooding the room with light from the hall beyond, and her mother came in on a little flurry of words. 'Too dreadful, darling. I've just been on the phone to Marricks to order some more coke—the boiler isn't nearly as hot as it should be, and Miss Meakins was complaining about the bathwater again this morning—and some thoroughly unpleasant person told me that unless something was paid on account, there wouldn't be any more deliveries. What do you think of that?'

Morgana shrugged. 'It's not entirely unexpected. We were never a good credit risk, and now that we've even lost the house . . .'

'Oh, Morgana,' Mrs Pentreath wailed, 'don't say such things!'

'But it's true.' Morgana's tone held a faint impatience. 'We can be dispossessed at any time by the new owner. You know the terms of the entail as well as I do. Mr Trevick made them more than clear.'

'But it's so unfair! And I'm sure it can't be legal—not in these days when people are always making such a noise about sexual discrimination.'

Morgana allowed herself a slight smile as she looked at her mother. 'An interesting point,' she conceded drily. 'But if we can't muster enough cash for the fuel bill, I doubt whether we could afford a lengthy court action.' Her gaze went to the bureau in the corner which she knew was stuffed with unpaid bills, and a number of receipts, including her father's subscription to the local golf club. When Martin Pentreath, big, bluff and genial, had been alive his choice of priorities hadn't seemed quite so curious, and his lack of responsibility about money matters had seemed almost endearing. Now they had assumed the proportions of a nightmare.

Elizabeth Pentreath sank down upon the elderly sofa. 'But it is unfair,' she repeated. 'Why, that awful Giles hadn't the slightest interest in Polzion. I'm sure he only kept the quarrel going with your grandfather so that he could keep away from the place, and use that as an excuse. After all, he went off swearing that he'd never set foot in the place again.'

'Well, he's kept his word,' said Morgana, her mouth twisting a little. 'Unless he comes back to haunt the house—and the new heir.' She moved away from the window and sat down beside her mother. 'Did Daddy never mention the entail to you?'

'Oh, years ago, when we first married, but he didn't want

to discuss it, and I could never find out any details. And when you were born, he talked of it again—spoke of trying to get it legally removed, but again I think it was a matter of cost which prevented him. And you know yourself, darling, how difficult it was to get him to talk about serious matters—especially when they concerned the quarrel. He didn't really want Giles' name mentioned at all.'

'I'm quite aware of that.' Morgana remembered with a pang her father's burst of temper whenever unwary references to the past had been made. From local gossip and what snippets she'd been able to piece together, she gathered that the quarrel had begun over a generation before when her grandfather and his cousin Mark had fallen out for reasons which had never been fully established, but with such bitterness that Mark had taken himself off from Polzion, never to be seen there again. Years later, his son Giles had returned in an attempt to heal the breach, but there had been more trouble and the re-opening, it seemed, of old wounds, and it had been Giles' turn to storm off, shaking the metaphorical dust of Polzion from his shoes for ever.

There had been generations of Pentreaths at Polzion. They had farmed the land, and mined for tin and copper, living well on the proceeds, and building this large rambling house to remind the world that in this corner of it they still ruled. But when the tin and copper petered out, so did the Pentreath fortunes, and now all the land, except an acre of overgrown garden round the house which enabled the hotel to advertise as 'standing in its splendid grounds', had been sold, even the Home Farm which Morgana's grandfather had clung to almost desperately.

It was only after his father's death that Martin Pentreath had conceived the idea of turning the family home into a hotel—something he frankly admitted he would never have dared to do or even mention when his father was alive. The fact that Polzion was relatively isolated, and could boast none of the amenities of the usual tourist traps and beauty spots did not trouble him in the least.

Morgana said, 'How Grandfather would have hated to

think of Mark's grandson inheriting this house!'

Her mother said hopefully, 'Perhaps he won't want it. Perhaps he'll—renounce the entail—or whatever one can do.'

'Whether he wants it or not, it belongs to him,' said Morgana. 'What a pity he wasn't born a girl, or that I wasn't a boy. It would have saved a lot of trouble and inconvenience all round. At least we wouldn't be hanging around here like this, waiting to be turned out of our home by a complete stranger. And I still think it would be more dignified to have packed and gone, instead of waiting here for sentence to be carried out.'

Her mother shuddered. 'You make it sound revolting, darling! But how could we possibly have left? There are the guests to consider.'

'Miss Meakins and Major Lawson,' Morgana said drily. 'Hardly a cast of thousands.'

'Well, it is the off-season,' Mrs Pentreath said defensively.

Morgana sighed. 'Even in the height of summer, Polzion House Hotel was never exactly an "ongoing situation".' She reproduced the jargon phrase with distaste. 'People on holiday want hot baths and swimming pools, and meals which aren't quite so dependent on the whim of the cook.'

'Elsa's a very good cook,' Mrs Pentreath said reproachfully.

'Oh, indeed she is, when the wind's in the right quarter, or the tea-leaves have looked hopeful, or the cards aren't presaging doom and disaster.'

'Well, she has got the sight,' Mrs Pentreath offered pacifically.

'Then I wish she'd "seen" the big freeze last winter. We might have been spared some burst pipes.' Morgana sounded defeated, and her mother said briskly,

'No wonder you're moping, darling. It's so gloomy in this room, and cold too. Why on earth didn't you make up the fire? It's nearly out.' She got up, bustling over to the hearth and stirring the reluctant embers with the long brass-handled poker.

Morgana shrugged. 'His electricity. His logs. Maybe we

shouldn't waste them.'

'I cannot believe any Pentreath would deny his own kin anything as basic as a fire to warm themselves by,' Mrs Pentreath protested.

'He's a stranger to us. We know nothing about him—except his name and the fact that he was too busy in America on some business deal to come to Daddy's funeral.' Morgana sounded suddenly raw. 'And since then, not a word, except this curt communication from his lawyers that he would be arriving here today.'

'I think that must be a mistake, don't you?' The fire revived to her satisfaction, Elizabeth Pentreath sat back on her heels and regarded her daughter. 'It's getting so late. It's almost dark, and the letter did say he would be here this morning.'

'Perhaps his car's broken down. Or maybe someone's been fiddling with the signpost again, and he's taken the wrong turning and driven straight along the cliff path into the sea.'

'Morgana!' Mrs Pentreath's hand clutched at her throat. 'You mustn't say—you mustn't even think such things. Do you think we should telephone the farm—get a search party organised?'

'No, I don't.' Morgana shook her head. 'He'll turn up. Bad pennies usually do.'

'You sound as if you don't care.'

'Frankly, I don't. Do you really expect me to?' Morgana's voice deepened passionately. 'This—Lyall Pentreath—he's an outsider, an intruder. He doesn't give a damn about Polzion. He's probably never been anywhere near Cornwall in his life. All he knows about us will be what he's heard from his father and grandfather, and that will probably be lies. There's never been any love lost between the two sides of the family. The only reason he's coming here now is to take possession of his inheritance, such as it is, lock, stock and barrel. And our feelings in the matter won't be of the slightest concern to him.'

'You can't really say that, darling. You don't know him.'

'Exactly the point I'm trying to make,' Morgana

argued. 'I don't—neither of us knows him. And he doesn't know us. But don't you think, in the circumstances, he might have made the effort?'

'He's in a difficult position,' her mother began, and Morgana snorted impatiently.

'And we're not? After all, we're the ones who stand to lose everything. And he's the winner who takes all. Well, in my book, he should have made contact before this. Long before. And the fact that he hasn't makes him a moral coward.'

'You're not being very logical.' Mrs Pentreath sounded plaintive. 'You're blaming him for coming here at all in one breath, and now he's on the way, or presumably so, you're complaining that he wasn't here days ago.'

'Not days. Weeks, months, years—when Daddy was alive,' Morgana said bitterly. 'When it might have done some good. We could all have talked—made plans, perhaps. Mummy, have you really thought what we're going to do? He may want us to leave immediately.'

'I can't believe that.' Mrs Pentreath's tone was depressed, and Morgana gave her a swift glance which mingled compassion with faint irritation.

Elizabeth Pentreath had led a sheltered life, in spite of the fact that there had never been much money. She had always been cossetted by her husband, which was all to the good in some ways, her daughter thought drily, but not so hot when it came to attempting to make her face reality.

Now, with an air of determination, Elizabeth rose and went round the room, switching on the lamps. There was a central pendant chandelier, but this was rarely used. For one thing, it used too much electricity, and for another in the lamps lower wattage bulbs could be used which helped to disguise how shabby the carpet and furnishings really were. As the hotel guests used this room for afternoon tea, and after dinner, this was a consideration, although Martin Pentreath had always worked on the lordly 'What's good enough for us is good enough for them' principle. It was a point of view which Morgana had never shared. She felt the family should have used another room, so that the drawing room could become a hotel lounge proper, where the guests could say whatever they liked without being inhibited by the presence of the proprietor and his family.

Miss Meakins might allow her eyes to fill with sentimental tears now that Martin was no longer leading the after-dinner conversation, but she had become increasingly voluble about faults in the service at Polzion House in the last two weeks, Morgana had noted drily. Not that most of the complaints weren't fully justified. She and Major Lawson might have been attracted to Polzion because the winter rates were more competitive than similar establishments in Eastbourne or Torquay, but they still expected the usual amenities of hotel life.

And in the past few weeks, life at Polzion had become increasingly difficult. Probate for Martin Pentreath's will had been applied for, but Mr Trevick had warned dourly that there would be little money left when outstanding debts were settled, though there were a couple of small insurance policies from which Elizabeth would benefit. Martin had made no large-scale provision for his widow and daughter, but then, as Morgana was forced to admit, he had always seemed so indestructible, like the Cornish granite his house was built on. Remembering her father, she thought it likely he had meant to leave them provided for—one day, when it could no longer be avoided, in much the same spirit as he'd stuffed unpaid bills in the bureau.

Morgana groaned inwardly as she thought of them, and she suspected her mother's reception at the coal-merchant's could well be the first in a long line of similar refusals. No coke meant that the ancient boiler would eventually go out altogether, and she doubted that even a further reduction in their 'competitive terms' would reconcile their guests to cold water, so she and her mother stood to lose their small remaining amount of direct income.

But that, she reminded herself, would be lost anyway as soon as the unknown Lyall Pentreath arrived. She imagined he would have already learned that his inheritance was being run as a small country hotel, and she found herself wondering what his reaction had been.

Contempt? Probably. Anger? Almost certainly. Perhaps Miss Meakins and the Major would also find themselves dumped bag and baggage into the damp chill of an October evening.

Except, as her mother said, that the new owner would hardly be coming now. He would be here in the morning to look over his new possession in daylight. Until now, they had counted each day at Polzion as a reprieve. Now, it seemed, they were reduced to hours.

Suddenly restless, she rose to her feet. 'I'd better go and see about tea. It's past the time already.'

'I expect Elsa has been waiting, dear, for your cousin to arrive.'

'My cousin.' Morgana repeated the words almost incredulously. It was the first time her mother or anyone else for that matter had used them in relation to Lyall Pentreath. It seemed alien and uncomfortable to think that this stranger was actually of her blood, even though the relationship between them was a remote one. Because of the quarrels and the separation between the two sides of the family, the other Pentreaths might as well not have existed as far as she was concerned.

'I wish they hadn't,' she thought fiercely, digging her nails into the palms of her hands as she left the room. 'I wish none of them had ever been born.'

The passage leading to what in happier days had been known as the servants' quarters was draughty, and Morgana shivered a little as she made her way down it. But the kitchen was warm, thanks to the big old-fashioned range—which also burned coke, she remembered dismally—on which Elsa produced delectable meals when she was in the mood.

What her mood was like today was anybody's guess. Breakfast and lunch had been passable, but there were no noticeable preparations for dinner, Morgana noted sinkingly. Instead, Elsa was sitting at the kitchen table staring down at a worn pack of cards spread there.

'Come in, maid, and shut the door,' she said absently without looking up.

'We were wondering about tea,' said Morgana, unable

to resist a curious glance down at the cards as she passed the table.

' 'Tes all ready, and the kettle's on the boil.' Elsa was built on generous lines, and her dark hair, liberally streaked with grey, was pinned back from her face with an incongruous selection of plastic hairslides in various colours and designs. Green butterflies and pink poodles were in favour that particular day, forming an unusual contrast to her bright blue overall, safety-pinned across her massive bosom. 'And I've made a batch of scones along with the cake,' she added sombrely.

'They look lovely.'

Elsa snorted. 'Can't go by looks. They'm sad, same as this 'ouse is sad. Same as these cards.' She gestured at them. 'Grief and misery, pain and woe, my lover—that's what's in store. And a fair man,' she added as something of an afterthought.

'Well, that's something,' said Morgana. 'At least it won't be Cousin Lyall. Pentreath men are always dark.'

'That's as mebbe,' Elsa said with dignity. 'But there b'ain't no dark man coming into your life, maid, not so far as I can see.'

'Then perhaps he really has driven over the cliff,' Morgana said cheerfully. 'Make the tea, Elsa darling, while I put the food on the tray.'

Whatever secret sorrow the scones might be nursing, they looked almost sprightly to her, she thought, as she picked up the plate, and the saffron cake which was one of Elsa's specialities was golden-brown and mouthwatering.

'About dinner——' she began tentatively.

'Funny ol' bit of meat the butcher sent.' Elsa was at the range, busy with teapot and kettle. 'Calls it beef, but I dunno. Looks tough as ol' boots to me.'

'Oh dear!' Morgana wondered privately whether the butcher was taking some kind of subtle revenge for an unpaid bill she hadn't discovered yet. 'Do you suppose pot-roasting would make it more tender?'

'I daresay.' Elsa set the teapot on the tray with an uncompromising thud. 'But I don't need any young maid to teach me my business in my own kitchen.'

'Of course not, Elsa darling.' Morgana's smile held its first real hint of mischief for some time.

'That's better,' Elsa said with rare approval. 'Now go and change out of that damned ol' frock before that young man gets here.'

'I'll do nothing of the sort.' Morgana lifted her chin and her green eyes flashed. 'It's perfectly suitable. This is the dress I got for Daddy's funeral.'

'Looks like the next funeral it goes to should be its own,' Elsa sniffed. 'But please yourself, though I can't see no sense going round looking like something the cat dragged in. You'm not a bad-looking maid when you try.'

'I'd better go before you turn my head completely,' Morgana said lightly as she picked up the tray.

'No danger of that, I reckon.' Elsa's fierce gaze softened as they swept over the girl's slim figure. 'You don't fancy yourself like some I could mention.'

Morgana hid a smile as she carried the tray out of the kitchen. Elsa was not usually so forbearing, and Morgana could only attribute her unusual delicacy this time to the fact that up to the time of the funeral she herself had been seeing a great deal of Robert Donleven, and might react with hostility to any overt criticism of his sister—because she was well aware that Elaine Donleven was the subject of Elsa's veiled remark.

Yet if she was honest, she had to admit that Elaine wasn't one of her favourite people either, though she would have been hard put to it to say why. Ever since Elaine had come to live at Home Farm and help Robert run the riding stables there, relations between the two girls had been perfectly civil, but no more.

Perhaps it was inevitable it should be so, she thought as she went along the passage. After all, the Donlevens had bought the Home Farm, as Robert's mother had made smilingly clear on more than one occasion, as an interest for her husband when he retired from being 'something' in the City of London. In the meantime it was run by an efficient manager, and Robert and his sister had started the riding stables there, again as a hobby rather than a living. Morgana felt sometimes that Elaine mentioned this

rather more than was strictly necessary, as if to emphasise
the gulf between those who had to work, and those for
whom the world was a playground.

Apart from exchange trips to France and Germany when
she was at school, Morgana's holidays had been spent in
and around Polzion, and she sometimes could not contain
a little surge of envy when she heard Elaine talk so carelessly of skiing at Klosters, and beach parties in the
Bahamas. Nor did it help to feel, as she often did, that
Elaine intended her to feel envious.

Robert, on the other hand, was very different. For one
thing his hair was inexorably sandy, instead of being deep
auburn like Elaine's, but his temperament was far more
unassuming than his sister's, and he took the day-to-day
running of the stables far more seriously than she did,
although ironically, Elaine was a spectacularly better
rider. But then, Morgana thought, she did not have his
patience with beginners.

For herself, she enjoyed Robert's company. She liked
him, and suspected that given time her feelings could
become much warmer. Ever since the funeral, he had been
assiduous in his attentions, sending her flowers, and phon-
ing nearly every day. She was grateful for this, and a little
relieved too, if she was honest. The Donlevens had always
been charming to her, but she had been aware all the
time in little ways that they felt Robert could do better for
himself than the daughter of a country hotelier. Now that
it was public knowledge in the area that, since her father's
death, the long-forgotten entail had come into force and
that soon she and her mother would probably be not only
penniless but probably homeless as well, she had wondered
whether any kind of pressure would be exerted to persuade
Robert to let their relationship slide.

If so, it clearly hadn't worked, or had had the opposite
effect, she thought, smiling a little as the image of Robert's
pleasant regular features and clear blue eyes rose in her
mind. And of course he was the fair man Elsa had seen in
the cards and he was going to propose to her and take her
away from all this.

She was grinning to herself as she carried the tray into

the drawing room, but the grin faded a little as she encountered the gaze of Miss Meakins, sitting bolt upright on the edge of her usual chair, clutching her knitting bag as a drowning person might clutch a lifebelt. Miss Meakins was elderly, and harmless, and Morgana felt sympathy for anyone whose life was a succession of cheap hotels, but she found Miss Meakins passion for attempting to be unobtrusive a trial. 'Without wishing to be a nuisance ...' and 'I wonder if I might ...' preceded even the most normal of requests and she seemed to spend most mealtimes in a state of permanent agitation.

A hotelier's lot is not a happy one, Morgana thought grimly as she set down the tea tray.

'Have you any idea where the others are, Miss Meakins?'

'Major Lawson usually goes for a walk before tea,' Miss Meakins said primly.

Major Lawson, Morgana thought, wasn't daft. She and her mother sometimes wondered about him. They usually had two or three permanent guests each winter at Polzion House, but Major Lawson wasn't in the usual mould at all. When his booking had originally been received, her father had been inclined to pooh-pooh his rank, saying he had probably been a clerk in the stores who had decided to promote himself after discharge. 'Or a con man,' he added cynically. But Martin Pentreath had been wrong.

Major Lawson was a tall, quietly spoken man, but there was an indefinable air of command about him. His clothes were not new, but their cut was impeccable, and the suitcases he'd brought them in were leather, and had been expensive. But in many ways he was an enigma. When pressed, he would talk about Army life, but he spoke in generalities with a certain diffidence. And he was a loner. Miss Meakins' flutterings had not the slightest effect on him. He enjoyed walking, and he spent a good deal of time in his room, working on a small portable typewriter. He was very tidy about his work, whatever it was. They'd only found out about it by chance, through Miss Meakins—'Not wishing to be any trouble, dear Mrs

Pentreath, but the constant tapping ... comes so plainly through the wall.'

Her eyes had gleamed with curiosity as she spoke, but it was doomed to be unsatisfied. Major Lawson had never volunteered why he spent several hours each day typing, and none of the Pentreaths were prepared to ask him. In the end Major Lawson was moved to another room, well out of earshot—to Miss Meakins' secret chagrin, Morgana suspected.

Quite suddenly she knew she had to get out of the house for a while. It was ridiculous, because it was almost dark, and almost certainly raining, but she needed to breathe fresh air and be completely alone for a while. Since her father's death, she had been rarely alone. Her mother had needed her and there were always things to be done, and at first she had welcomed this because it meant there was less time to think, and to worry and ask herself what she was going to do. But now, when there was so little time left for thinking and planning, she had to get away on her own for a while. It had been building up inside her all day, this need to be alone, to escape. That was why she had felt so restless earlier.

She flashed a brief smile at her mother as she passed her in the doorway. 'I'm going out for a little while.'

'Just as you please, dear,' Mrs Pentreath responded.

Morgana went into the hall and on into the small cloakroom which opened off it. Her old school cape was there, and she swung it round her shoulders, pulling the hood up over her cloud of dark hair. As she re-emerged into the hall, the telephone rang, and she crossed to the reception desk to answer it.

'Polzion House,' she said crisply.

It was a relief to hear Robert's quiet 'Hello, darling. Just ringing to find out how everything went today. What's he like?'

'Your guess is as good as mine. He didn't show up.'

'Well, that's pretty cavalier,' Robert was plainly taken aback. 'Wasn't there even a message?'

'Nothing at all. We've spent the whole day on tenter-hooks, and all to no avail.'

'I suppose he could have had an accident,' Robert said slowly.

'We thought of that.' Morgana laughed. 'And at this moment he's breathing his last at the foot of Polzion cliffs. I wish he was,' she added hotly.

It was Robert's turn to laugh. 'Darling, what a little savage you are! It's a good job my respected mama can't hear your fulminations.'

'Meaning her worst fears would be fully justified?' Morgana asked coolly, then relented. 'I'm sorry, Rob. Your mother can't help the way she is, any more than I can. And I won't say anything shocking in front of her, I promise. I'm just a little uptight over this whole business, that's all. And the atmosphere in the house is deadly at the moment—Elsa prophesying doom all over the place, and Mummy's trying to be optimistic and see a silver lining in everything. I was just going for a walk when you rang.'

'In the direction of the Home Farm?' he enquired hopefully.

She sighed. 'Not really. I do need to be on my own for a time. You understand, don't you?'

'I'll try to anyway,' he said cheerfully. 'You know I'm here if you need me. Perhaps I could pick you up later when you've walked your blues off, and we could have a drink somewhere.'

'Now that would be nice,' she said. 'See you.' She was smiling as she put the receiver down. Robert was sweet, she thought, and she'd forgotten to tell him he was the fair man that Elsa had seen in the cards, but it didn't matter. Gems like that would keep, and she would enjoy telling him later, over their drink.

As she went out of the house, closing the side door carefully against the gusting wind, Morgana wondered why she hadn't considered going down to the Home Farm, because until Rob had mentioned it, it hadn't even crossed her mind to do so.

Was she being totally fair to him? she wondered. He wanted to help. The phone calls proved that. He was kind and concerned, and he'd been furious when he heard about the entail, calling it a 'load of outdated nonsense and prejudice'. And although she agreed with every word, it wasn't what she wanted to hear right now.

Nor did she really want to hear him ask her to marry him, which she suspected he might do. If and when he proposed, she wanted it to be for the right reasons, and that was quite apart from the fact that deep in her bones she felt they didn't know each other well enough yet.

Of course, it might be that they would never know each other well enough. She and her mother might have to leave Polzion and go miles away, and eventually, inevitably, the gap that she and Rob had left in each other's lives would be filled with other people. Journeys led often to lovers' partings as well as their meetings, she thought with a little grimace. And 'lover' was a strong way of describing Rob, although she enjoyed the moments she spent in his arms. He was a normal man with all the needs which that implied, but he was not overly demanding. He preferred to let their relationship proceed steadily rather than sweep her off her feet into a headlong surrender they might both regret later.

. But if she went to him now, with all her doubts and her troubles, he might interpret her need for comfort and reassurance rather differently, and that would simply create more problems.

'And just now I have as many as I can handle,' she muttered against the moan of the wind.

She buried her hands in the pockets of her cape, her fingers closing round the familiar shape of her small pocket torch, and it was that which decided her where to go for her walk. Her original intention had been to follow the lane round, perhaps even as far as the village, but now she knew she wanted the open spaces of the stretch of moorland behind the house. Even in summertime, it seemed bleak, the few trees bent and stunted under the power of the prevailing westerly gales, but Morgana loved it, in particular the great stone which crowned its crest.

It was an odd-looking stone—a tall thick stem of granite with another slab balanced across its top. In some guide books it was referred to as the Giant's Table, but locally it was known as the Wishing Stone because it was said that

if you put your hand on the upright and made a wish, and
then circled the stone three times, the top slab would rock
gently if the wish was to be granted. At all other times, of
course, it was said to be immovable, but Morgana had
always thought that a really desperate wisher could
probably give fate a helping hand with a quick nudge at
the cross-stone.

Sometimes she'd wondered if there had once been other
stones there, so that the hillside above Polzion had resembled Stonehenge or Avebury, until people had come and
taken them for building. Yet it was intriguing that they
had left this one, and she had asked herself why often.
Maybe it was because they sensed its power, or more pro-
saically perhaps it was because the cross-stone had proved
more difficult to shift than anticipated.

Anyway, there it stood, like a mysterious signpost to a
secret in the youth of mankind, surviving the initials which
had been carved on it, the picnics which had been eaten
in its shadow, and all the attempts of vandals to dislodge
it, squat and oddly reassuring in its timelessness.

As she picked her way across the thick clumps of grass
and bracken, the wind snatched at her hood, pulling it
back from her head, and making her dark hair billow
round her like a cloud. She breathed deeply. This was
what she had wanted—the freshness of damp undergrowth
and sea salt brought to her on the moving air. Rob would
think she was mad if he could see her now, she thought,
stumbling a little on a tussock of grass, but then he hadn't
been born here as she had. In fact she'd often wondered
what had prompted his father to buy the Home Farm in
the first place. Perhaps under his rather staid appearance
he was really a romantic at heart, remembering the pull
of the boyhood holidays he mentioned so often. Certainly
Morgana doubted whether his wife's wishes had much to
do with his decision. Mrs Donleven's roots seemed firmly
grounded in the Home Counties.

Morgana was out of breath by the time she reached the
wishing stone. The wind had been blowing steadily against
her all the way, and by all the natural laws the stone
should already have been rocking precariously on its pedi-

ment. But it wasn't, of course. She leaned against the upright, regaining her breath, and looking about her. She could see the lights of Polzion House below her, and away on the right those of the Home Farm. She couldn't see the village, because it was down in a hollow in the edge of the sea, where the surrounding cliffs provided a safe harbour for the fishing and pleasure boats.

She thought suddenly, 'This could be the last time—the very last time that I stand here.' She put her hand on the stone and it felt warm to the touch, but perhaps that was because she herself suddenly felt so cold.

It couldn't happen, she told herself passionately. This was her place, her land, and she refused to give it up to an uncaring stranger.

She said quietly, but aloud because that was the rule, 'I wish that he may never come here. I wish that he may renounce his inheritance, and that we may never meet.' Then she began to walk round the stone, slowly and carefully, the wind whipping her cloak around her legs, her head thrown back slightly, her eyes narrowed against the gloom as she watched for a sign of movement.

She had never really believed in the Wishing Stone, had always dismissed it as an amusing local superstition, but now she desperately wanted the legend to be true, and to work for her.

But when her circuit was completed, the great stone remained where it was implacable, immovable. Her wish hadn't been granted, and she could have thrown herself on to the ground and wept and drummed her heels like a tired child.

She stared at the stone, and sighed despairingly, 'Oh, why didn't you work?'

And from somewhere behind her, but altogether too close for comfort a man's voice said, 'Perhaps you used the wrong spell. Or simply asked for the wrong thing.'

Morgana spun round, her hand going to her mouth to stifle an involuntary scream, and found herself caught, transfixed like a butterfly to a cork, in the merciless, all-encompassing beam of a powerful torch.

CHAPTER TWO

HER heart hammering, Morgana stared back, lifting her chin defiantly. She didn't recognise the voice. Low-pitched and resonant, with a trace of an unfamiliar accent, it struck no chord in her memory. And she couldn't see him either, although she had the impression that he was tall.

She wondered why she hadn't heard him approach, but supposed it had been partly because of the noise of the wind, and principally, because she had been so totally absorbed in what she was doing. All of which he had observed, judging by his opening remark. She felt the blood rush into her face with embarrassment, and her temper rising at the same time as she visualised him skulking up through the bracken, deliberately not using his torch, giving her no hint that she was no longer alone until it was too late, and she had made a complete and utter fool of herself.

She demanded sharply, 'Do you enjoy spying?'

'Not particularly, although I must confess it can be most instructive,' he said. 'And it's not every day one gets the paces. But isn't it a little early for this sort of thing? I always understood the witching hour was midnight.'

There was a trace of amusement in his voice which he wasn't at all concerned to hide, and it stung.

She said stiffly, 'I am not a witch.'

'I think that's just as well.' The laughter was open now. 'I don't think you'd be very good at it. That stone's supposed to rock, isn't it?'

'How did you know that?'

'From a book I bought in the village. I hope you didn't think it was a closely guarded secret.'

'No, no, of course not.' The fright he had given her, and her own anger, had knocked her slightly off balance, and she hated the way he kept her trapped in the damned beam of light, so that he could see her, but she could know

23

nothing about him, except that impression of height.

Her voice sharpened. 'Did your book also tell you that this is private land?'

It was only a technicality, and no one at Polzion House had ever dreamed of debarring any of the interested tourists from visiting the stone, but there was something about this man that flicked her on the raw, that made her want to put him down—to make him feel small in his turn. It was abominable the way he had stood there in the darkness and watched her, and listened, and then added insult to injury by laughing at her.

He said slowly, 'Is it now? And do you think the owner would mind?'

'We don't like trespassers round here—intruders.'

'I was always told the Cornish were very hospitable. And as for intruding, actually I was here before you. I was standing back so I could look at the stone from a distance when you appeared out of nowhere and began your incantations.'

'I had every reason to believe I would be alone,' she said coldly. 'And do you think you could switch off that spotlight of yours—always supposing you have seen all that you want,' she added with icy sarcasm.

The torch remained on. He said, 'Tell me something—are you always so prickly? Even in that weird cloak with your hair all over your face, you're an attractive girl. You must have had men look at you before this.'

'Oh, yes,' she said. 'But I've always been able to look at them too. The present situation is a little too one-sided for my taste.'

He said, 'But easily remedied.' The torch beam swung up and away from her and she saw him properly for the first time. He was tall, his face thin, with prominent cheekbones, a high-bridged nose and firm mouth and chin. And his hair was fair, lighter altogether than Rob's, and longer too, reaching almost to the collar of the black leather coat he was wearing.

Morgana thought, 'A fair man—but it can't be . . . it couldn't be! I don't believe it.'

As if he could read her thoughts, he began to smile,

deep laugh lines appearing beside his mouth.

'You look as if you've seen a ghost.'

She wanted to ask, 'Who are you?' but the words wouldn't come. Then the torch snapped off, and there was only the darkness and the howl of the wind, and the tall dimly seen figure who said quietly, 'And perhaps you have, at that.'

He was coming towards her, and she recoiled involuntarily, her hands flying up in front of her to keep him away. Then she stumbled against a clump of grass and went flying.

'Dear God!' The torch flicked on again, as she lay there, winded and humiliated, and he bent towards her pulling her up, his voice abrupt as he asked, 'Have you hurt yourself? Are you all right?'

'I'm fine.' She'd twisted her ankle slightly and it hurt enough to make her wince when she put her weight on it, but she wasn't going admit it. She didn't want him to touch her again. He'd put his hands under her arms and lifted her as if she was a child, and she'd hated it.

He said harshly, 'When I said you'd seen a ghost, I wasn't trying to frighten you. There was no need for you to leap away like that. What I meant was that I thought I possibly reminded you of someone.'

Morgana could have said quite truthfully, 'You remind me of a number of people. You remind me of at least half the portraits hanging in the long gallery at home, except that they're all dark, and you're fair.' But she remained silent because there was still an outside chance it might all be a coincidence, and she could be wrong. Under her breath, she prayed that she was wrong.

He said sharply, 'Well?'

She shrugged. 'I don't spend my life looking for chance resemblances to people I know in local tourists. We have too many of them.'

'I wasn't talking about chance, and I think you know it.' His hand gripped her arm, bruising her flesh, and she said with ice in her voice, 'Would you let go of me, please?'

'When you've answered a few simple questions. For

starters, what's your name?'

'If this is a new version of the pick-up, then I'm not impressed,' she shot at him.

'I'm tempted to make a very different impression on you.' His voice slowed to a drawl, but now he didn't sound amused at all. The torchlight was on her face again, and his hand moved from her arm to grip her chin. She wanted to pull away, but she wasn't sure she could evade his grasp, and it would be another humiliation to struggle and lose. So she remained very still, making her eyes blank, enduring his scrutiny.

At last he said slowly, 'I'm Lyall Pentreath. And unless I miss my guess, you're my cousin Morgana.'

'Brilliantly deduced,' she said huskily. 'And what are we supposed to do now—shake hands?'

'I think it's a little late for that.' His voice was dry. 'We expected you this morning.'

'I was held up.' He let her go and stepped back, and her breath escaped with a little gasp of relief.

'More business, I suppose.' She made no attempt to hide the bitterness in her voice.

'Of a sort.'

'I suppose it didn't occur that my mother and I would be waiting for you—would be worried?'

'Frankly it didn't.' A match flared as he lit a cheroot, his hands sheltering the flame against the snatching wind, and she saw his mouth twist cynically. 'I hardly imagined I would be the most welcome visitor the Polzion House Hotel had ever had.'

She'd heard the edge in his voice when he mentioned the word hotel, and she made her own tone blank and a little wondering. 'You resent the fact that the family home is now a commercial enterprise? I'd have thought as a business man yourself, you'd have been delighted.'

'But then,' he said coolly, 'I would hardly describe that particular venture as a commercial enterprise.'

Morgana was silent for a moment, her brain working madly. Far from lacking interest in his inheritance, it now seemed he was only too well informed. But where had he gleaned his information? she wondered. Was that where he'd been since this morning? Going round Polzion, asking questions? She flinched inwardly as she thought of some of the answers he might have been given. On the other hand, it was far more likely that he'd found out all he wanted to know through correspondence between his solicitors and Mr Trevick, who would have been been bound to be frank.

She decided to proceed cautiously. 'I admit we're not the Hilton, but we make out.'

'Do you really? You seem to be alone in that opinion. From what I've learned, the hotel seems to owe quite a lot of money to a number of people.'

She was mortified, but she made herself reply quietly. 'Yes—we do, unfortunately. But it's been a bad year.'

'It must have been a succession of bad years if all I've been told is true.'

'If you want to put it that way,' Morgana agreed, numbly hating him.

'I don't, believe me.' His tone was dry. 'After all—a hotel in surroundings like these. It's hard to see how it could fail.'

'In the course of your snooping, you may also have noticed that Polzion isn't exactly Newquay,' she said sharply. 'I'm sorry if we haven't come up to your expectations, but no doubt you'll be able to figure out the reasons why at your leisure.'

'Unfortunately, I don't have that much leisure to waste.' He sounded abrupt again. 'I'm going to walk down to the house now, and meet your mother. Are you going to come with me, or have you got more spells to cast?'

'No,' she snapped. 'I'll come down with you.' She felt chilled to the bone, and cold and sick inside.

'Good. I didn't relish the prospect of being turned into a frog as soon as I turned my back.'

'I think in the circumstances,' she said tightly, 'a rat would be more appropriate.'

'If we're playing at animal similes, I can think of one or two that would fit you quite well too,' he returned equally, and Morgana flushed in the darkness. After a moment's pause he turned away and moved off down the hill, without waiting to see if she was following or not. Morgana gritted her teeth and went after him, fumbling in her cape pocket for her own torch. It couldn't compete with the powerful beam that his flashlight was sending out, but at least it gave her an illusion of independence.

He said over his shoulder, 'Be careful you don't fall.'

'Thanks for the advice,' she snapped, 'but I do happen to know every inch of these moors.' And remembered too late that he'd had to haul her up from the ground only a few minutes before.

'Then perhaps you'd like to go first. My own acquaintanceship is only just beginning,' he said silkily.

'That,' she snapped, as she went past him, her chin in the air, 'is entirely your own fault.'

She walked ahead of him as fast as she could go, determined not to stumble again or make a fool of herself in any other way, although every instinct was screaming at her to run and never stop until she reached Polzion House and safety. When she reached the road she made no attempt to wait for him to catch up with her, but simply marched along as if he had ceased to exist for her. Nor did he try and draw level, so he obviously had as little desire for her company as she had for his, she thought defiantly.

She didn't pause or look back until they reached the front door, and she opened it and went into the hall. Her mother was at the desk, just putting the telephone down.

'That was Mr Trevick, darling. The Pentreath man is in the area—he called at the office earlier today. Where can he have got to, do you suppose?'

'Here,' Morgana said grimly, and stepped aside.

Lyall Pentreath walked forward, and she took her first good look at him. All the impressions she had received up by the Wishing Stone—the height, the fairness—were reinforced, and more beside. His face was deeply tanned, accentuating the strong lines of nose, mouth and jaw, and his eyes were a deep and piercing blue. The black leather coat covered a roll-necked sweater in the same shade, and light grey pants, fitted closely to lean hips and long legs.

Elizabeth Pentreath said helplessly, 'Oh dear!'

He said quietly and without mockery. 'This is a difficult

occasion for us both, Mrs Pentreath, and anything I say is liable to be misunderstood. I wish we could have met in different circumstances.'

He had charm, Morgana supposed bitterly, watching her mother's face flush slightly with pleasure as he took her hand. And the cynical lines of his mouth told her that he was quite well aware of it, and knew how to use it to its best effect. She stood and watched, and hated him for it. Hated him for the elegance of his expensive clothes and the slight drawl with which he spoke. Everything about him told of a world very remote from their own small part of the Cornish peninsula. He looked, she thought frankly, as if he'd never actually known what a hard day's work was, never had his hands dirty in his life, and she despised him for it.

Effete, she thought. A lady's man. A desk-job Romeo. I bet the typing pool's little hearts go pit-a-pat whenever he saunters through.

Mrs Pentreath said, 'Would you come into the drawing room? We've just been having tea. I'll ask Elsa to make some fresh and . . .'

He lifted a hand. 'Not for me, thank you. I don't really have a great deal of time.' He glanced at the plain gold watch on his wrist. 'I have to pick up my car and get back to Truro.'

'Oh.' Elizabeth Pentreath was taken aback. 'Then you're not staying? I've had a room prepared here for you.'

'Not this time around, I'm afraid.' His smile removed any hint of a rebuff. 'But when my immediate plans are finalised, perhaps I can take advantage of your kind offer.'

'Oh, I'm sure you'll do that.' Morgana muttered rebelliously, and received a horrified look from her mother.

When Mrs Pentreath turned to lead the way into the drawing room, Morgana suddenly felt her arm seized in a paralysing grip.

Lyall said softly and evenly, 'I'm doing my best to ease the situation, sweetheart, so stop bitching, otherwise I may take advantage of you in a way you won't like. Anyway, the only person you're hurting is your mother.' He let her go almost contemptuously, and walked unhurriedly away. Morgana watched him go, but she didn't follow. Instead she almost ran down the passage to the kitchen.

Elsa was standing at the deep enamel sink, washing up, but she glanced round as Morgana flew in.

'Dear soul,' she remarked. 'Where's the fire to?'

'It's him. He's here.' Morgana sank down on to a chair beside the kitchen table, unfastening her cape, and pushing it back from her shoulders.

'Well, better late than never, they do say,' Elsa said comfortably, subjecting a plate to a minute inspection before placing it on the drying rack on the draining board.

'I don't say it.' Morgana pushed her hands through her dishevelled hair, lifting it away from the nape of her neck. 'Oh, Elsa, he's vile! And he's fair,' she added.

'The cards don't lie, my lover. A fair man, they said, and pain and woe.'

'He's that all right,' Morgana said petulantly. 'Oh, what are we going to do?'

'As we're told, I daresay.' Elsa held out a tea-towel with an inexorable air. 'No point in fretting without reason, neither.'

Morgana accepted the cloth with a little sigh and began to wipe the dishes. 'You can hardly say we have no reason,' she objected.

'What I say is it's best we wait and hear what the genn'lman says before we start calling 'um names,' Elsa returned.

'I don't want to hear anything from him,' Morgana said passionately. 'But at least he's not staying the night here—that's something to be thankful for. I can't bear the thought of having to share a roof with him, even for one night.'

From the doorway Lyall said drily, 'Do you think you could bear to share it for long enough to show me a little of the house? Your mother is otherwise occupied, or I wouldn't trouble you.'

The cup she was drying slipped from her hands and

smashed into a hundred fragments on the flagged floor.

'Now see what you've done!' Elsa scolded. 'Of all the clumsy maids! Don't go treading through it, making things worse neither. Tek no notice of her, sir,' she added to Lyall who stood watching, his face expressionless. 'She'm mazed with worry, that's all. She don't mean half of what she says.'

'Even the half is more than sufficient.' He walked into the kitchen, ignoring Morgana, who had fetched a dustpan and brush from the broom cupboard and was sweeping the fragments into it with more scarlet-cheeked vigour than accuracy. 'You must be Elsa, the mainstay of this establishment.' He smiled. 'Mrs Pentreath's own words, not gratuitous flattery from me, I promise you.'

'Mrs Pentreath's a nice lady.' Elsa wiped a damp hand on her overall and shook hands with him. 'And the late master was a well-meaning genn'lman. More than that I can't say.'

Lyall was looking around him. Watching him under her lashes, as she dumped the broken crockery into the kitchen bin, Morgana was resentfully aware that she was seeing the kitchen through his eyes—the big old-fashioned sink with its vast scrubbed draining board, the range, the enormous dresser which filled one wall, in all its homely inconvenience.

He said almost idly, 'It must be hell having to cope without a dishwasher in the height of the season.'

'Tesn't wonderful, that's true.' Elsa allowed graciously. 'But we manage. And hard work never hurt no one.'

'How right you are.' He glanced at Morgana. 'I suggest as we're here, you may as well begin by showing me the rest of the kitchen quarters. I take it that this isn't the only room.'

'No.' She would rather have cut her throat with one of Elsa's brightly honed knives than have shown him a shed in someone else's garden, but she gritted her teeth. 'There is a scullery—through here. I suppose these days, you'd call it a utility room. The washing machine's in here, and another sink, and the deep-freeze.'

'At least there are those,' he observed, glancing round,

his brows raised. 'What about a tumble-dryer? How do you manage the laundry in wet weather?'

'There's a drying rack that works on a pulley in the kitchen. We've always found it perfectly efficient,' she said coldly.

'But then,' he said smoothly, 'the hotel has never precisely operated at full stretch, has it?'

'As you say,' she agreed woodenly. 'That door leads to a courtyard, and the former stables. Do you want to look at them now? They're rather dilapidated.'

'I can imagine. Is there electricity laid on?'

'Well—no.'

'Then I'll save that particular delight for another occasion. What kind of garden is there at the rear?'

She said reluctantly, 'Beyond the stables there's a walled area which is quite sheltered. We grow vegetables there, and soft fruit, but not to any great extent.'

'And use the home-grown produce in the hotel dining room?'

She was a little taken aback. 'Well, sometimes. We don't grow all that much. There are a few apple trees as well.'

Lyall gave a sharp sigh. 'Perhaps we'd better look at the rest of the ground floor rooms—leaving the drawing room out of the tour. I've had enough of the stares of the curious.'

'I suppose you think we should have told our guests to go,' Morgana said defensively.

'I didn't say that.'

'No—but you obviously don't want them here. Only it is—or it has been our living, and we didn't hear from you, so we didn't know what to do for the best.'

His mouth curled sardonically. 'That last phrase I'd say sums up the present situation pretty accurately. Now, might we get on, please? As I've pointed out, my time here is limited.'

Oh, that it were true, Morgana thought in impotent rage leading the way along the passage to the dining room.

Lyall said little as she did the honours of the house in a small remote voice—like a bored house agent with a reluctant client, she realised with unwilling humour, as she heard herself uttering phrases like 'original mouldings' and 'local stone'.

She tried to look at him as little as possible, so it was difficult to gauge his reactions to what he was seeing—to know whether he was impressed, appalled, or simply indifferent. One of his few abrupt questions was about central heating, and she had to confess there wasn't any, but that they'd always fround the open fires perfectly adequate. It wasn't true. Her mother had bemoaned the lack of radiators on innumerable occasions, but Morgana wasn't prepared to admit that. As far as this—interloper was concerned, the present occupants thought that Polzion House was perfect, warts and all.

Besides, she didn't want him to like the house. The solution to all their problems would be for him to refuse the inheritance, and he could just do that, if there were sufficient drawbacks. She could imagine the kind of accommodation that would appeal to him—some chic penthouse, she thought impatiently, with wall-to-wall carpeting, and gold-plated bathroom fittings, to go with his gold-plated image.

As she led the way up the broad, shallow curve of the staircase, her sense of purpose faltered a little. At the head of the stairs was the long gallery off which the principal bedrooms opened, with smaller wings at each end, and in this gallery the family portraits were hung. However much she might silently condemn him as an intruder and a stranger, she could not escape the fact that every few yards they were going to come face to face with his likeness, and it wouldn't escape him either.

She made no reference to them as they passed, but took him straight to the master bedroom which her parents used to share, and where Elizabeth Pentreath now slept alone. He looked around it without comment, opening the door into the small dressing room which lay off it.

'Are the guest rooms similar?' he asked, when they were once again on the gallery.

Morgana hesitated. 'Well, usually guests have a choice of rooms. We charge different prices for them, of course. At the moment Miss Meakins has accommodation in the

West Wing, but we moved Major Lawson over to the other side because of his typing.' He said nothing in response, and after a minute she added defensively, 'There's nothing wrong with the rooms in the wings. We always show the guests everything that's available.'

She walked on quickly down the corridor, and Lyall followed.

He said, 'Just a moment. Haven't you forgotten something?'

She stopped and turned quickly. He was standing by a door, touching the handle, his brows raised interrogatively.

She said reluctantly, 'Oh—that's my room.' She half expected him to leave it, and follow her, but he remained where he was.

'I suppose you want to see it.' She made no effort to disguise her resentment.

'I want to see everything. I thought I'd made that clear.'

Yes, you did, she thought, as she walked back. And you're also reminding me that this isn't really my room any more. That it belongs to you, like everything else here, and that I'm only occupying it on sufferance. As if I could forget that, even for a moment! I just—hoped that you wouldn't insist.

Her hand was shaking as she turned the handle and pushed open the door, fumbling for the light switch. Every step he'd taken in this house was an invasion of privacy, but this was the worst of all.

She had always slept in this room, from being a small child. Her whole life was laid out here for anyone to see. At a casual glance, Lyall could find out anything he wanted to know—could see the books, from childhood fairy tales to modern novels, which crammed the bulging bookcase—the worn teddy bear still occupying a place of honour on the narrow window seat—even the scent she used, standing on her dressing table, and her nightdress folded on the small single bed with its virginal white candlewick coverlet.

As it was, his glance was far from casual. He walked into the centre of the room and stood there, his hands buried deep into the pockets of the black leather coat he hadn't bothered to remove. And he took everything in, while Morgana waited in the doorway, feeling as humiliated as if she'd been forced to strip naked in front of him.

It was deliberate, she knew that. Next time and every time that she entered this room, he intended her to remember his presence there, his scrutiny covering all her most personal possessions, lingering on the narrowness of the bed, while a half-smile played about his mouth which she had not the slightest difficulty in interpreting.

She thought, 'Damn you!' and was aghast to see his smile widen, and realise she had spoken her thought aloud.

He said softly, 'It's nice to know, darling, that one's efforts are appreciated.'

She said, 'When you've finished your—inventory, I'll be in the corridor.'

He joined her there almost immediately. 'I have to admire your choice of sanctuary,' he observed rather mockingly. 'I imagine that in daylight, the view from the window is quite spectacular.'

'Yes—you can see the sea from all the second floor windows on this side.' Her voice sounded stilted.

'And I presume that the eyes I can feel watching me along this gallery are those of our mutual ancestors?'

'Yes,' she agreed resignedly.

'Are they not included in the guided tour?'

She shrugged. 'As you pointed out, they are our mutual ancestors. You probably know as much as I do.'

He said softly, 'And you know that isn't the truth. So suppose you tell me about them.'

There was a note in his voice which sent little prickles of apprehension running along her skin, like a storm warning. There was a brief, crackling silence, then she said, 'Very well. The man on your left is Josiah Pentreath. He built most of this house at the height of the tin-mining industry, but it's always been reckoned he built the stables out of his profits from smuggling. He had two sons, Mark and Giles—they're over there. Giles didn't just follow in his father's footsteps, he overtook him. This has always been a bad coast for wrecks, and Giles is popularly supposed to have done his share in encouraging them. He's one of the Pentreath black sheep. Mark, on the other hand, was converted to Methodism by John Wesley.' She paused, then said, 'Mark and Giles—and Martin too—have always been Pentreath names.'

She didn't have to add, 'But Lyall isn't.'

He said, 'I was named for my mother's family. You can hardly blame my father for dispensing with family tradition under the circumstances.'

Her voice lacked expression. 'I suppose not. Anyway, those rather downtrodden-looking ladies you see are their respective wives.'

He said almost sharply, 'She doesn't look downtrodden at all.'

'Which one are you looking at?' Morgana peered. 'Oh, I didn't mean that one. She's my grandmother.'

'Not one of the mutual ancestors,' he said slowly. 'She was very beautiful, wasn't she? May I ask why she's got up like a medieval princess?'

'There was some sort of Arthurian pageant going on, and she was playing the part of Morgan le Fay.' She was reluctant to complete the story, but she didn't want him to probe either, so she went on doggedly, 'That was where Grandfather saw her, and he fell in love with her at first sight. After they were married, he insisted on having her portrait painted in her pageant costume. They had no daughters, only one son—my father, and he made him promise that if he had a daughter he would call her Morgana.'

'And here you are.'

'Yes,' she said tightly, 'here I am. Grandfather was still alive when I was born, and he was so delighted to have the little girl he'd wanted at last.'

'Having no idea, of course, that you'd be an only child. Quite one of life's little ironies.'

'You could put it like that.' She bit her lip hard. 'Do you want another instalment of family history, or shall we look at the rest of the bedrooms? There are the attics as well.'

'I think the attics will have to be saved, along with the stables for my next visit,' he said, glancing at his watch. 'I must go. Purely as a matter of interest, you understand, which room was I to have been given?'

'We'd put you in the East Wing,' she mumbled.

Lyall lifted a sardonic brow. 'I understood all guests were allowed a choice.'

Morgana shrugged again. 'The same rule would have applied.' She took a deep breath, forcing the words to her lips. 'After all, they're all your rooms—now.'

'Yes, they are, aren't they?' he said silkily. 'It's just as well I decided to stay in Truro instead. I don't think you'd have liked my choice, Morgan le Fay.'

For a moment she looked at him uncomprehendingly, then as realisation dawned, an angry flush invaded her cheeks.

'That wouldn't matter,' she said untruthfully. 'As I shall have to move out eventually anyway, it may as well be sooner than later.'

He laughed, his eyes going over her in one swift, sensuous appraisal. 'Who said anything about moving out?'

Her flush deepened. 'How dare you?' she stormed.

'Oh, I dare,' he said. 'When you get to know me better, you'll be amazed how much I dare.'

'I haven't the slightest wish to know you better. I only wish I'd never had to meet you at all.'

'I gathered that when I heard you casting your spell on the moor,' he said mockingly. 'Also when I overheard you bemoaning the fact that you had to share a roof with me. I enjoy a challenge, and it occurred to me that it might be amusing to persuade you to share far more than just my roof.'

'You're out of your mind,' she said bitingly. 'Or perhaps your unexpected inheritance has gone to your head. It's the house and its contents which belong to you. I don't.'

He said very gently, 'But you will, Morgan le Fay. You will. Because in spite of your little spells and maledictions, I'm here, and I intend to stay.'

He took one quick stride forward and pulled her into his arms, his mouth stifling her instinctive cry of protest on her lips. There was no mercy in his kiss, nothing exploratory or tentative, just an immediate hungry demand, which, against her will, against all her instincts aroused an eventual, shaming response. And at once he let her go, as if her capitulation had been all he'd been waiting for.

Morgana shrank back against the wall, her hand going up to cover her bruised mouth, too furious to speak, too shocked to know what to say. And the worst of it was that Lyall was smiling at her.

'You bastard!' she choked eventually.

'From what you tell me, I come from a long line of them,' he said coolly. 'But I'm glad to know that you're not the downtrodden sort. I'll see you tomorrow, Morgana.'

'I'll see you in hell!' she raged.

His mouth twisted. 'Hell's only the flip side of Paradise. Sometimes it's hard to differentiate between the two, as you may find, my little witch.'

She whirled past him, into her room, and slammed the door. She leaned back against the panels, her breathing quick and shallow, her small breasts rising and falling as if she'd been running.

She didn't know whether to scream, or burst into tears, and was sorely tempted to do both, because it was just as she'd feared. Lyall might at this moment be on his way to Truro, but this room was filled with him. She could close her eyes, and blot out his image, but that couldn't destroy the taste of him, the scent, the feel of his body against her own.

For as long as she stayed in this house, she knew she would never be alone again, and the knowledge made her tremble.

CHAPTER THREE

MORGANA was still lying on her bed staring sightlessly up at the ceiling almost an hour later when there was a knock at the door, and her mother popped an apologetic head into the room.

'Darling, are you all right? It's almost time for dinner. Are you coming down?'

Morgana forced a smile. 'I don't think so. I—I'm not really very hungry, and Rob is picking me up later. We'll probably go to the Polzion Arms and I can grab a sandwich there.'

'You're probably more than wise.' said Mrs Pentreath with a little sigh. 'Elsa's behaving very oddly, and she won't even discuss whether there's going to be a dessert. I suppose if all else fails we can open some tinned fruit.' She paused. 'Well, what did you think of him? Really, he seemed very pleasant.'

'That's hardly the word I would use.' Morgana swung herself to the floor and walked across to the dressing table.

'Well, darling, it's hardly any wonder. You were extremely rude to him. I was very dubious about allowing you to show him round, but Miss Meakins was being extremely difficult—most inquisitive, and so carping about all sorts of little things which she's *never* mentioned before, and all done for effect, I'm convinced. So I was really grateful to Mr Pentreath when he made a tactful exit.' She hesitated. 'Did he give you any kind of hint—about his intentions, I mean?'

Morgana, brushing her hair, had an insane desire to burst into hysterical laughter.

She said gently, 'No, love. At least, not in the way that you mean. I don't know what his plans are.'

Mrs Pentreath sighed again. 'He's coming back tomorrow, so I've no doubt he'll tell us then. I've invited him to lunch, and told Elsa to get a couple of ducks out of the freezer.'

'I don't think you'll soften his heart with our brand of gastronomic delights.' Morgana said drily. 'He has an expense account air about him.'

'Well, I must say I liked him much better than I expected to.' Mrs Pentreath's voice was slightly defensive. 'He isn't a bit like his late father—or what I remember of him at least. He must take after his mother's side of the family. I wonder who Giles did marry?'

'Does it matter?' Morgana wearily replaced her brush on the dressing table. 'It would have been far better for us if he'd remained a bachelor.'

'I wonder if Lyall himself is married?' mused her mother. 'Did he mention a wife, or a fiancée?'

On the contrary, Morgana thought bleakly, but that doesn't mean with his kind that neither of those ladies exists.

Aloud she said, 'We didn't really talk about personal things. He wanted to see the house, and learn something about the family history. I told him about Giles the Wrecker.'

'That's a terrible story,' Mrs Pentreath said indignantly. 'I've never believed one word of it.'

'Yet you believe that old Josiah was a smuggler.' Morgana shook her head affectionately.

'Well, smuggling is different,' Mrs Pentreath excused herself. 'In those days, simply everyone did it. It was quite respectable.'

'Tell that to the Customs and Excise!' Morgana gave her mother a swift hug. 'Shall I lay the dining table, or has Elsa done it?'

'She was doing it when I came upstairs, and singing 'Rock of Ages' very loudly, and rather badly. I think this business over the entail has affected her almost as deeply as it has us.'

'Nonsense,' Morgana said robustly. 'She's wallowing in it. She's seen a fair man, and grief and woe in the cards, and she's in her element. We ought to start calling her Cassandra instead.' She caught her mother looking at her oddly, and demanded resignedly, 'Now what's the matter?'

'Nothing really, dear, except—oh, Morgana, that awful

dress! I know it's a mark of respect, but poor Daddy would have loathed it so. Such a depressing colour, and it doesn't even fit you very well. I don't know what your cousin must have thought.'

Morgana gave her reflection a rueful look. 'I think it's probably served its purpose,' she conceded. 'I'll give it to the next jumble sale. But I couldn't care less what Lyall Pentreath thinks about me, or my clothes,' she added defiantly. 'For two pins I'd wear the beastly thing every time he comes here.'

Mrs Pentreath shuddered. 'Spare the rest of us, darling! And you couldn't possibly wear it to go out with Rob.' She gave a little sigh. 'I'd better go downstairs and face the inquisition again. One can understand their concern, I suppose. This is as much their home, temporarily at least, as it is ours.' She gave an uncertain little smile, said, 'Have a lovely time, darling, and—don't worry. I'm sure everything is going to work out for the best,' and went out of the room.

Morgana pulled off the despised dress and let it fall in a heap on the floor, before padding across to the wardrobe and viewing the contents. In the end, she decided to wear a pair of dark red corded jeans, and a cream Shetland wool sweater with a high collar. She had always liked simple clothes, and that was just as well, she thought wryly. She had found at school that she had a flair for dressmaking, and she had always ensured that the garments she made never had a home-made air, although nothing she wore could ever compete with the clothes of Elaine or Caroline Donleven, who bought many of their things from couture houses in London.

Robert had already arrived when she went downstairs and was standing in front of the drawing room fire, chatting to her mother. Miss Meakins had disappeared, she was relieved to notice, presumably to dress for dinner. Only Major Lawson was left, sitting quietly near the fire, completing the *Times* crossword. He glanced up as Morgana entered, and rose, giving her his pleasant, rather shy smile, and she thought, not for the first time, what a nice man he seemed, and what a pity all the guests they'd had staying at

Polzion House over the years couldn't have been like him.

She said a swift goodbye to her mother, then she and Robert walked out to where his car was parked at the front of the house.

'I hear your unwelcome visitor arrived after all,' Rob said casually as he opened the passenger door for her.

'Yes, he did.' Morgana tried to keep her tone non-committal, but was aware, just the same, that an edge had crept in.

'Was he as you expected? Your mother seems to have been quite charmed.'

'Mummy always tends to meet everyone more than halfway.' Morgana said ruefully.

'I gather that you weren't equally captivated?' Rob smiled.

'I found him loathsome,' she said coldly.

'Good,' he approved. 'From your mother's remarks, I'd begun to think I might have reason to be jealous.' It was said teasingly, but there was an underlying serious note.

'No reason at all,' she said. She was glad the darkness in the car hid the sudden surge of colour in her face as she remembered unwillingly that uncontrolled response to his kiss that Lyall had forced from her. It made her feel sick with self-disgust to recall it to mind. If it had been a chance encounter, in some ways it would have been easier to forget, but Lyall had the right to return to Polzion House whenever he wanted, and every time she saw him, she was going to be haunted by the remembered searing pressure of his mouth on hers.

She asked lightly, 'Where are we going?'

'To the Polzion Arms. Mum and Dad have come down for the weekend, and they're having dinner there. They've asked us to join them.'

'Oh, lord!' Morgana was aghast. 'Why didn't you warn me? I'd at least have put on a skirt.'

'You look terrific just as you are,' he said. 'My cool, practical lady.'

Cool and practical! She could have laughed out loud. What would Rob have said if he could have seen her a couple of hours earlier, prancing round the Wishing Stone like a superstitious idiot, or boiling with tension and temper as she led Lyall Pentreath round the house she could no longer claim as her home? She'd made a fool of herself in every way there was, she thought, but she wouldn't allow it to happen again. The next time she saw Lyall Pentreath, she would have herself well in hand. She would build a high wall around her emotions and retreat to a safe distance behind it—and whatever he threw at her, whether it was sexual innuendo or the rank injustice of the legal situation they found themselves in, then she would take it, coolly and practically. She wasn't going to crumble at the knees because a man who undoubtedly had already had more than his fair share of success with women had made a pass at her.

Rob asked suddenly, 'What is it, love? You're as restless as a volcano about to go into eruption. Do you want to go home and change, because there's time . . .'

'No,' she said hastily. 'I'm sorry, Rob. It's been an upsetting day, taken all round. I—I do need to relax.'

The Donlevens were already sitting in the firelit comfort of the lounge bar when Rob and Morgana arrived. Morgana saw drily that she wasn't the only one wearing trousers, although the contrast between her own simple garb and Elaine's aquamarine silk tunic and tightly cuffed harem pants could hardly have been greater. As she murmured the conventional greetings, Morgana was aware of the other girl's eyes flicking over her in rather contemptuous satisfaction. She accepted the dry Martini which Mr Donleven offered her, and sat down on the high-backed wooden settle which flanked one side of the log fire, making herself relax, forcing herself to smile a response to Mrs Donlevan's remarks, knowing full well that Elaine's scrutiny had become speculative.

Eventually she spoke, breaking rather impatiently across her mother's comments about the harvest of apples from the Home Farm's orchard, 'Did the missing heir turn up then?'

'Yes, eventually.' Morgana's tone was short, and she picked up her drink and sipped it.

'The whole thing sounds so incredibly unlikely.' Elaine's eyes were fixed on her face. 'It all sounds like the plot for one of those old-fashioned romances.'

'Well, I can assure you that there's little of the old-fashioned romantic about my cousin Lyall,' said Morgana, and instantly regretted it, because Elaine's gaze sharpened with interest.

'Dear me,' she drawled. 'Have the sparks been flying already?'

'I hardly think that's any of our business, Elaine,' her father broke in repressively.

Elaine shrugged unrepentantly. 'That doesn't make it any less fascinating,' she said. 'On the contrary. So what's he like, Morgana? Tall, dark and handsome?'

'He's tall,' said Morgana, keeping her voice deliberately cool. 'And I suppose some women might find him attractive.'

'But not you?' Elaine probed.

'Certainly not her.' Rob laid a hand over Morgana's and smiled at her possessively. 'Morgana only has eyes for me, haven't you, love?'

Out of the corner of her eye, Morgana saw his mother glance at them quickly, then away, confirming her suspicions that Mrs Donleven would not break her heart if Morgana was forced to move far away from Polzion, and well out of Rob's orbit. She wished suddenly that it was possible for her to lean across the narrow oak table that separated them and say, 'Look, you have nothing to worry about. I like Rob enormously, but I'm not in love with him. Even if I'd been my father's heir, I would still feel the same.'

But she and Mrs Donleven had never been on terms of sufficient intimacy for her to even venture on such a comment. Besides, it was hardly the topic for a supposedly pleasant social occasion, and she had no wish to hurt Rob, although she supposed it was inevitable that their parting would be accompanied by a certain amount of pain, less on her side than on his, she was forced to acknowledge, and found herself wondering why she should suddenly be so sure of this.

She took the menu Elaine handed her with a condescending smile and studied it, the neat copperplate in which it was written dancing meaninglessly in front of her eyes.

'Well,' said Elaine, 'attractive or not, he certainly seems

to have given you food for thought.'

'Is it any wonder?' Morgana countered lightly. 'He's now the legal owner of the house I live in. If someone arrived to dispossess you tomorrow, I imagine you'd also be a little on edge.'

'It's a bad business.' Mr Donleven shook his head. 'Did you really have no idea what would happen? Didn't your late father give you any kind of warning?'

As Morgana shook her head, she reflected that Martin Pentreath hadn't been the kind of man who dealt in warnings, merely in optimism which was generally unfounded.

'From what I can gather from our solicitor, my father preferred to ignore the other branch of the family altogether. For some reason, he genuinely believed that Giles Pentreath had died a childless bachelor. Of course, if he had done so, or if his child had been a daughter as well, then everything would have been entirely different.'

Mr Donleven sighed and drank some of his whisky. Morgana could guess what he was thinking, that if he had been in Martin Pentreath's shoes he would have done everything possible to discover the truth beyond all doubt, and then taken some kind of action to protect his family from the eventual blow. There was little excuse to offer for her father's ostrich-like behaviour, she thought sadly.

Rob bent solicitously towards her. 'What would you like to eat, love?'

'Oh—melon, I think, and fillet steak.' She put the menu down. 'I'm not very hungry.'

Mr Donleven gave the order to the hovering waitress, then turned back to Morgana. 'Has your cousin given any indication of his plans for the house? Does he intend to live there himself?'

'I don't know.' Morgana shook her head. 'But I would have thought it was unlikely.'

'You mean he might be prepared to sell?' Mrs Donleven broke in rather too eagerly, and Morgana turned an astonished look on her.

'Mother!' Rob's frown was thunderous. 'You know we agreed we wouldn't say anything.'

'Say anything about what?' Morgana said rather desperately, and Mr Donleven leaned forward conciliatingly.

'Oh, it was just an idea that my—that we had.' He gave her an uneasy smile. 'We've always admired the house, you know, and we thought if it was coming on the market at the right price . . .'

'Because it could be made charming,' his wife intervened, and then flushed as if it suddenly occurred to her that she had been less than tactful.

'Yes, it could,' Morgana agreed wryly, thinking of the expensive transformation that had overtaken the Home Farm in recent years. But although it had become a charming, and even luxurious home, she supposed she could have guessed that it would only ever be second-best in Mrs Donleven's eyes while Polzion House was only a mile away. She sees herself as the lady of the manor, she thought, and what a fool I was not to see it coming.

'Well, what do you think?' Rob asked her eagerly, and she turned a rather blank look at him.

'About what?'

'About the possibility of our buying the house.'

She gave a defensive shrug. 'It isn't really any of my business,' she parried. 'Any discussions would have to be with the new owner and his solicitors.'

'Well, I know that, of course.' There was a dawning puzzlement in Rob's eyes as he studied her. 'But how would you feel about it, Morgana? That's important too. And it would be a solution, wouldn't it?'

A solution to what? she asked herself stupidly. All she could see were more problems, proliferating like weeds, and judging by the fleeting expressions of alarm she had noticed on the faces of both Mrs Donleven and Elaine, she guessed that although they might covet Polzion House, the prospect of her permanent company there, presumably as Rob's wife, had as little appeal for them as for her.

She sought to temporise. 'I don't really know what to say. It's all been rather a shock.'

'Of course it has,' Mr Donleven interrupted soothingly. 'We shouldn't have mentioned it. This is neither the time nor the place.' He gave his wife a warning glance, then determinedly changed the subject, leaving Morgana to pursue her reeling thoughts.

Polzion House was like a carcase with the vultures clustering round it, she told herself almost hysterically. Suddenly she couldn't wait to get away. Mr Donleven, she knew, was a wealthy man, and could undoubtedly afford to pay any inflated price that Lyall Pentreath might place on the property. But the idea of Mrs Donleven and Elaine in particular queening it there was oddly abhorrent. And Rob must be mad to think she would ever seriously contemplate sharing her old home with his mother and his sister, she thought confusedly.

Even if they all thought the world of each other, it would be a difficult situation. As it was, it would be impossible.

At that moment, the waitress came to tell them their table was prepared. Morgana could not say that she particularly enjoyed the meal that followed, but Mr Donleven did his best to lighten the atmosphere with some amusing anecdotes of personalities in the City with whom he was in almost daily contact, and which to Morgana were merely names in the newspaper, or faces on television. She found his accounts of board-room coups and averted take-overs less than fascinating, but she appreciated his attempts to keep the conversation away from more personal issues.

She was quiet as they drove back to the house later, and she deliberately evaded all Rob's hints that she should invite him in for coffee or a nightcap. As she passed through the hall, she noticed that the lights were still on in the drawing room and could hear the murmur of voices beyond the closed door. She sighed noiselessly. She had hoped her mother would be alone, so she could tell her about this new and unexpected development. As it was, she felt she would rather go up to her room without a word to anyone. She certainly couldn't face a room full of guests, or cope with the sort of speculation that Lyall Pentreath's visit would have aroused.

She went up the stairs as silently as a ghost, her feet floating over the familiar treads. The gallery was full of shadows, but they had never troubled her enough to prompt her to switch on the light, and they did not do so now. From the shadows, the eyes of the dead Pentreaths watched her.

And what will happen to you when the Donlevens take over? she thought. They were only family portraits, after all, and she doubted whether they had any real value. There were certainly no Gainsboroughs or Reynolds concealed among them to arouse the interest of their new owner, so eventually they would find themselves dismissed to a saleroom or an attic, she decided despondently. It was too much to hope for that she could find a home for them, as well as for herself and her mother.

Tomorrow, she supposed, it would have to begin—the hunt for a job. There was residential work, she knew. She'd seen the advertisements many times in a national magazine. If her mother could obtain a post as a house-keeper, she herself would be more than willing to work as a maid, if it meant they could stay together. Housework, after all, was something she was well used to, and she had never found it a great hardship.

She went slowly into her bedroom and stood looking round her, at the familiar shape of the walls and window, the outlines of the furniture, breathing the hint of her own scent in the air. Her own—and something else as well. The dark, bitter smell of stale tobacco smoke.

Her mouth tightened in fury. She might have known that the room would still harbour the essence of him. He'd left his mark on it, in the same way as he had on her.

She marched over to the window and yanked it open, allowing the night wind to billow in. The cold stream of air made her shiver, and long after, hours later as she lay in the darkness, the window safely closed again, the coldness was still there deep inside her.

Morgana was sitting at the bureau in the drawing room, trying to put the papers there in some kind of order, when she heard the sound of the car the following morning. Momentarily she stiffened, knowing who it must be, but she made herself go on with her task. There had been a letter from Mr Trevick that morning, asking her to supply him with all the unpaid bills to date, and it was something she was anxious to get out of the way as soon as possible. The next unpleasant job, she thought, grimacing, would be to go through the rest of the things in the bureau with her mother and decide what should be kept and what should be thrown away. As it was, there were letters, receipts, old address books, diaries and even ancient Christmas and birthday cards all jumbled together in glorious confusion.

The small room off the hall which they had used as an office was rather more presentable, but then she and her mother had kept the accounts between them, and Martin Pentreath had rarely been in there, except when he couldn't find something, so there had been little opportunity for him to spread his own particular brand of chaos there.

When the imperative sound of the front door bell shrilled through the house, she made no attempt to go and answer it, and presently she heard Elsa go grumbling past.

I wonder he didn't just open the door and walk in, she thought. Her mother, she knew, was in the office at this moment, rather nervously assembling all the keys she could find. Morgana had no idea what she intended to do with them—arrange a little handing-over ceremony, presumably.

She was frankly amazed when Elaine's voice said from the doorway, 'Working hard as always, sweetie?'

Morgana swung round on her chair, her expression mirroring her utter bewilderment, as Elaine advanced into the room, smiling. She looked amazingly chic in a moss green velvet suit, with dark green suede boots, and she was carrying a large bunch of roses.

'Is someone ill?' Morgana asked drily, and a tinge of colour came into Elaine's cheeks.

'Mummy thought your mother might like to have them,' she said hurriedly. 'They're about the last we shall have this season. I loathe the winter, don't you?'

'Not particularly.' Morgana rose from her chair. 'Thank you, Elaine. It was a kind thought on your mother's part,' she added with a trace of irony, knowing perfectly well the real motive for Elaine's unexpected visit. 'Would you like some coffee?'

'I'd adore some.' Elaine sank down on the sofa. 'That is if you're not too busy.'

'Not at all,' Morgana returned. 'It's almost time to make some for the guests, anyway,' she added over her shoulder as she went to the door.

In the kitchen, Elsa was already setting the tray with a face like thunder.

'What's Lady Fan Tod come visiting for, I'd like to know?' she demanded truculently.

'To bring Mummy some flowers.' Morgana laid the roses down on the kitchen table. 'Can you put them in water, Elsa, until I've got time to deal with them properly. They're very lovely—far better than anything our garden's managed to produce this year.'

Elsa snorted. 'Her and her blamed roses! She thinks she's the Queen of Hearts, that one, but there's darkness underneath, maid, you mark my words'.

When Morgana returned to the drawing room with the coffee, Elaine was on her feet, examining one of the china ornaments on the mantelpiece.

'Doing an inventory?' Morgana wanted to ask, but out of consideration for Robert she remained silent.

'Well, this is very nice,' said Elaine with patent insincerity, re-seating herself on the sofa, and smoothing a non-existent wrinkle out of her velvet skirt. 'I do hope I haven't called at a bad time. I know how—awkward things must be, just now.'

'It's very kind of you to spare us the time.' Morgana decided to outdo the other girl in insincerity. 'You're always so busy at the riding school.'

'Usually, yes,' Elaine allowed. 'But things are a little quiet just at the moment, and there's certainly nothing that Rob can't handle on his own,' she added with a touch of complacence.

'Yes, he's extremely capable,' Morgana agreed, pouring a cup of coffee and offering it to Elaine.

There was silence for a moment, then Elaine said, 'And what's going to happen to the incredible Elsa when you leave here? She's always been so devoted to your family, hasn't she?'

'A cook as good as Elsa won't have the slightest difficulty in geting another job,' Morgana returned steadily.

'You think she couldn't be persuaded to stay under a new régime?' Elaine sipped her coffee with evident appreciation.

Morgana lifted a shoulder. 'I haven't the slightest idea,' she said shortly. 'She's very much her own woman. You'd better ask her.'

'My dear, I wouldn't presume to do anything of the sort! She absolutely terrifies me,' Elaine laughed. 'Besides, it's early days yet for that sort of consideration. Particularly when none of us have any idea what plans your cousin may have. Has he tasted Elsa's cooking yet, by the way?'

'No, but we expect him here for lunch,' said Morgana with faint amusement, recognising how she had been manoeuvred into giving Elaine the information she wanted, and wondering at the same time what excuse the other girl would have for hanging about for another hour or more at Polzion House.

'Then he has a treat in store.' Elaine gave a brilliant smile.

Looking back, Morgana could only recall one occasion when Elaine had a meal at Polzion House. It was when she had first started going out with Rob, and he'd had some idealistic hope about the two girls becoming friends—a hope that had been doomed from the outset, Morgana thought, remembering Elaine's patronising air as she had studied both her surroundings and her companions.

The door opened and Elizabeth Pentreath came in. 'Why, Miss Donleven!'

She sounded so taken aback that Morgana had to stifle a grin. Out of consideration for her mother, who she felt had quite enough to worry her at the moment, she hadn't mentioned the conversation over dinner of the previous evening. Now she surreptitiously crossed her fingers that Elaine wouldn't refer to it either.

'Elaine has brought us the last of the roses from the Home Farm,' she announced. 'They're really beautiful.'

'What a kind thought,' her mother said politely. 'I always did envy the Home Farm its little rose garden—so sheltered in that hollow. Oh, is that coffee? How very nice.'

Morgana poured another cup and handed it to her mother, who had seated herself on the sofa. Elizabeth Pentreath gave her a frankly hunted look, 'Have—have there been any messages, dear?'

'Not so far.' Morgana tried to give her a reassuring smile.

'Oh well.' Mrs Pentreath looked at her watch. 'It's still quite early, of course. And he probably has other matters to attend to.'

Undoubtedly, Morgana thought bitterly. More snooping and prying in the locality.

Elaine asked, rather too casually, 'Have you any idea what he does?'

Mrs Pentreath shook her head. 'He mentioned nothing. In fact, he didn't really talk about himself at all. But he seems to have business on both sides of the Atlantic, so I imagine he works for some big company.'

'One would think so,' Elaine agreed. 'In other circumstances, of course, it would all be rather thrilling—discovering a branch of the family about which one knew relatively nothing.'

'I'd have been perfectly happy to remain in ignorance of this particular member of it,' Morgana said bluntly.

'Really?' Elaine studied her face with interest. 'Daddy was saying later last night that it's always better in these cases if things can be settled amicably.'

'Fortunately it has nothing to do with me,' Morgana said levelly. 'Mr Pentreath's negotiations will, naturally, be with my mother.'

That, she thought, had a reasonably dignified ring to it. The fact that there would be no negotiations was something that concerned only her and her mother.

'The whole thing is so deliciously Victorian,' Elaine purred. 'Entails—and male heirs. Of course, a hundred years ago he would probably have done the honourable thing and made you an offer of marriage, Morgana. If he's not already married, that is.'

'I've no idea whether he is, or not,' said Mrs Pentreath. 'He didn't mention anything about a wife—did he, Morgana?'

'Not a word,' Morgana shrugged. 'Although I suppose that doesn't mean a great deal, these days.'

Not to a man like him anyway, she thought. She'd assumed—his behaviour ·had led her to believe that he was unmarried—yet the opposite could be the case, which would make the way he had acted even more vile and insulting. The coffee tasted bitter suddenly, and she got up from her chair and replaced her cup on the tray.

'I think, if you'll excuse me, that I'll go and see to those roses,' she said abruptly.

'That's a good idea,' her mother approved. 'And perhaps you could check on lunch at the same time. Will you stay, Miss Donleven?' she added politely but without enthusiasm.

'I'd adore to, but Mummy's expecting me back,' Elaine gushed.

Good for Mummy, Morgana thought, as she walked along the passage to the kitchen. She was smiling to herself as she pushed open the door, but the smile was wiped from her face when she saw Lyall Pentreath sitting at the table, looking down at the spread of cards Elsa was busy laying before him.

'You?' Morgana exclaimed. 'But we didn't hear . . . How did you get here?'

He rose, and she was unwillingly made aware of his height and the lazy strength of his movements.

'I found the back entrance into the stable yard, so I left my car there,' he said. 'Why, have you any objection?'

'Of course not,' she denied colourlessly. 'You—you're free to come and go as you wish, naturally. I was just—surprised, that's all.'

'I seem to have done very little but startle you since we met.' His tone was pleasant, but his eyes were amused, challenging, and she resented the implications of the challenge. 'I shall have to try to do better in future.'

'I don't suppose we shall meet very much in future,' she said flatly. 'Elsa, you really shouldn't bother Mr Pentreath with that nonsense of yours.'

'Nonsense, is it?' Elsa sniffed. 'There's been times when you've been glad enough for me to look into the future for you.'

But that, Morgana thought, was when I felt safe and secure. When the future seemed a series of bright pictures—almost a game, and not the frightening reality that it's become.

Lyall Pentreath said, 'I asked her to read my cards. I understand that she has quite a reputation for it locally.'

Morgana shrugged. 'She does a guest appearance at the Polzion church fête each summer. It goes down well with the tourists.'

'But of course it's all superstition and you don't believe in it,' he said, and his smile told her that he was remembering their first encounter on the moor in the shadow of the Wishing Stone.

'I think we've already established that I'm probably as credulous as the next person,' she said curtly. 'Now, I suggest that we leave Elsa to get on with lunch. I presume you've come to tell my mother your arrangements for taking possession of your—property.' The words nearly choked her, but they had to be said.

'I've come to talk to your mother, yes.' His brows rose a little. 'Am I to infer that you haven't the slightest interest in hearing what I have to say?'

Morgana shrugged. 'It's really none of my business. I just want my mother spared any further anxiety.'

Lyall gave her a long look. 'Really? I imagine one of her major preoccupations right now must be you.'

Morgana was utterly taken aback. 'What on earth are you talking about?'

'Think about it,' he said succinctly. He swung back to Elsa, and smiled at her. 'Thanks for the reading. I'll be back for another one at a later date.'

'You'm more than welcome,' Elsa assured him, sweeping the cards into a pile, but not before Morgana had seen the Queen of Hearts occupying pride of place in the spread.

Irrationally, she found herself hoping that Elaine would have gone by now, but as they emerged from the kitchen passage into the hall, there she was, saying goodbye to Elizabeth Pentreath at the door, the watery sunlight turning her hair to a burnished aureole around her head.

Morgana heard Lyall catch his breath sharply.

Mrs Pentreath looked at her daughter, her brows raised in mute almost comical query as she saw her companion.

'Elsa was telling his fortune in the kitchen,' Morgana said shortly.

'How nice,' Mrs Pentreath murmured helplessly. 'Er— Miss Donleven, may I introduce our cousin Lyall Pentreath?'

Elaine moved forward, extending a hand, her full lips parting in a smile of candid assessment. 'Oh, but I think we've met already,' she exclaimed. 'Weren't you at Lindsay van Guisen's party at Gstaad last Christmas?'

'Yes, I was there.' Lyall took her hand and showed no sign of letting it go again. 'But if you're saying you were there, and I've forgotten, then I shall never forgive myself.'

Elaine laughed prettily. 'Oh, you were far too occupied with Lindsay—and who can blame you? She's a very lovely girl, and she has all that wonderful money. I'd say it was an irresistible combination.'

'I've managed to resist it so far,' he said rather drily. 'Lindsay's my stepsister.'

'Lucky Lindsay,' Elaine murmured, then she paused, her eyes widening dramatically. 'Stepsister? Oh, my God, then you must be . . .'

'Lyall van Guisen,' he supplied. 'I see you know the name.'

'Well, of course.' Elaine said tremulously. 'Daddy's company does endless business with the van Guisen-Lyall corporation. Good heavens, this is absolutely amazing! I can't wait to tell him.'

'Perhaps you'd also like to tell me,' Morgana interposed swiftly. 'Just what is going on here? We understood you were Lyall Pentreath, only now it turns out you're someone completely different.'

He gave her an almost indifferent look. 'My full name is Lyall Pentreath van Guisen. When my mother remarried some years ago, my stepfather asked if I would take his name. He was a fine man, and I was happy to agree. Is that sufficient explanation?'

'No, I'm damned if it is!' she retorted hotly. 'It seems to

me we've taken far too much on trust already. Have you any means of proving who you really are?'

He said wearily, 'I've already provided your lawyer with all the necessary credentials. What else do you want to know about? Birthmarks? I have none. And if you imagine for one moment I would go to the trouble of fabricating a claim to an estate which I know already is going to cause me nothing but problems, then you're crazy.'

'Be nice to him, Morgana,' Elaine advised, her smile widening. 'Most people would be glad to know they'd got a millionaire in the family. Owning even part of van Guisen-Lyall is like having your own private goldmine. I've often heard Daddy say so.'

Morgana could feel the colour draining out of her cheeks. 'A millionaire? You're actually a millionaire?' The blaze was starting in her voice.

He met her furious gaze, his own eyes cool and guarded. 'Yes—for my sins.'

'There's only one sin that concerns me,' she said savagely. 'The sin of stealing my mother's home and livelihood from her. No wonder you're a rich man! You'd probably stoop to pick a penny out of the gutter. My God, people like you make me sick!'

'Fascinating.' He returned ice to her fire. 'Remind me sometime to tell you what I think of people like you.' He turned to Elaine. 'I'm sorry you had to take part in our little family quarrel. It seems we've been noted for them for generations.'

'Oh, you mustn't be too angry with Morgana,' Elaine almost cooed. 'She's naturally upset about this whole situation.' She paused. 'Is this just a flying visit to Polzion, Lyall, or will you be staying for a while? I know Mummy and Daddy would love to ask you over for dinner.'

'I'll be staying,' he said, and for the moment his eyes met Morgana's.

She turned away, and walked blindly into the drawing room, her heart thumping painfully. That was more than just a challenge, she thought bitterly. It was a declaration of war.

CHAPTER FOUR

MORGANA walked across to the drawing room window and stood looking out. It seemed impossible to realise that only twenty-four hours had passed since she had stood there, dreading his arrival. It seemed like a lifetime, and her head reeled as she tried to make sense of all that had happened. Out in the garden, a few leaves still clung tenaciously to the trees, in defiance of the sudden gusts of wind that sent their fellows whirling and trembling to the ground. She thought, 'I know how they feel.'

In the hall she could hear the murmur of voices, and Elaine's laughter. She bit her lip angrily, condemning herself for having behaved as she had in front of the other girl. She'd intended to play it cool, but there was something about Lyall Pentreath that flicked her on the raw. But even that was no excuse for speaking to him as she had done in front of a stranger.

The door opened, and she looked round, expecting to see her mother's reproachful face, but instead Lyall entered alone, closing the door behind him. He stood looking at her in silence for a moment, and she quailed inwardly.

'Where's my mother?' she demanded.

'Organising coffee for the hotel guests in the dining room,' he said. 'I told her I'd like a few words with you in private.'

'To hear my apology for my bad manners?' she asked bitterly.

'I don't expect miracles,' he bit back at her. 'You're just one seething bundle of resentment, aren't you, lady? And you're used to having everything your own way. It's an unhappy combination, but if you were only affecting yourself by it, then I'd leave you to rot. But you're not the only one concerned. There's your mother. Hasn't she enough to contend with right now without worrying herself sick

57

about the next bloody thing you're going to say or do?'

'That's not fair!' she gasped furiously. 'I'd do anything that would help Mummy. She's my only concern in all this.'

'Then you have a strange way of showing it,' he said coldly. 'You feel you've been badly treated—well, you probably have a point. But just remember, my little witch, that I didn't invent this entail. To me it's an anachronism, and a waste of my time and money.'

'Oh, I thought it wouldn't be long before your money was mentioned,' she jibed. 'I'm sorry if I haven't been treating you with the respect your position deserves. Should we all pull our forelocks and call you Squire, perhaps? Only I should warn you that in these parts a man is judged by what he is, rather than by what he has.'

Lyall said without a trace of emotion, 'So I've been discovering. Would you like to know how your late father rated?'

For a moment she stared at him, then she said thickly, 'You bastard!' and started to cry.

'It seems you know already,' he commented. He moved away as she hunted blindly in her sleeve for her handkerchief. When she had regained command of herself, he was standing by the fireplace, his arm resting along the mantelshelf, and with one foot supported on the brass fender.

He said, 'Come and sit down, Morgana. We have some talking to do.'

She said huskily, 'I think we've said it all.'

'We haven't even started. Now, do you come here and sit on the sofa, or do I have to fetch you?'

Morgana moved hastily. The last thing in the world she wanted was for him to touch her again, and although obeying him even in this small way wasn't something she relished, nevertheless it seemed the wisest thing to do.

'That's better,' he approved unsmilingly. 'Now the first thing I have to say is that I've decided to take your mother up on her offer of accommodation. As I said before, I've only a limited amount of time at my disposal at present, and I want to be on the spot for the next few days while I put my plans for this house into operation.'

'So when do you want us to leave?' she asked. Now that the moment of truth had finally arrived, she felt strangely calm.

'Who said anything about leaving?' He turned his head and looked at her coolly.

'Well——' she floundered for a moment, nonplussed. 'We can't possibly stay . . .'

'You'll be surprised what you can do,' he said softly. 'Now, here comes your mother, so let's try and act as if we're not at each other's throats.'

Elizabeth Pentreath came into the drawing room on a little burst of apology. Miss Meakins had a complaint about the light switch in her room. 'And it has given trouble in the past, I'm afraid, although Martin did look at it once or twice.' She gave a little sigh. 'But he wasn't much of an electrician, I'm afraid.'

'I think he'd probably have to have been a genius to have made much improvement,' Lyall said drily. 'The whole house needs re-wiring, Mrs Pentreath. Surely you must know that?'

Elizabeth sighed again. 'Knowing it and being able to do something about it are two different things, I'm afraid. It's all been such a worry, and then people started making threatening noises about new fire regulations.' She shook her head. 'Oh dear!'

Lyall studied her for a moment, then he said quite gently 'Mrs Pentreath, do you actually like the hotel business?'

She brightened. 'Oddly enough—yes. Oh, I don't like the business side—trying to make silk purses out of sows' ears all the time, but I do like *people*. I like trying to make them comfortable—even the rather difficult ones like Miss Meakins, although she's only lonely, I think, poor soul.'

He said, 'Then I hope you'll listen to the proposition I have for you, Mrs Pentreath. As it stands, this place is frankly a white elephant. It's too big to be a family home these days, and it never had the injection of capital it needed to be a successful hotel. Now, I'm prepared to change all that.'

Morgana said slowly, 'You mean—you want to run it as a hotel?'

'Not quite. As it happens one of van Guisen-Lyall's subsidiaries owns a hotel chain, but I'm not proposing to add Polzion House to that. Winters in England rather preclude it from becoming one of the world's playgrounds. No, what I'm suggesting is rather different. I want to see a complete facelift—new wiring, proper heating, any repairs necessary, redecoration throughout—but nothing that's going to spoil its country house image. For most of the year it can continue to be run as an ordinary hotel, although I hope the improvements will bring in more trade, but there's one proviso—I want van Guisen-Lyall employees always to have top priority. In fact there'll be times when the place will probably be occupied by no one else.'

Mrs Pentreath said with faint bewilderment, 'I'm not sure I understand. You want to run Polzion House as a private hotel for the staff of your companies?'

'In a way. I also envisage holding company conferences here. People seem to think better, become more creative in a relaxed informal atmosphere. And I'd say this place is about as far from the rat race as it's possible to get. In between times—well, strain gets to everyone. I want a quiet refuge where members of our companies' staff can unwind.'

'A haven for tired business executives?' Morgana raised her eyebrows. 'Then I suppose your improvements should include a bar and a selection of hostesses.'

He didn't even glance in her direction. 'A bar, certainly,' he said shortly. 'But don't run away with the idea that there'll be only executives here. There are just as many pressures on the shop floor these days. And the majority of those who come here will be accompanied by their wives, so we can do without your other suggestion, well meant though I'm sure it was.'

Morgana flushed and relapsed into silence.

Lyall looked at Elizabeth Pentreath. 'Any comments? Do you like the idea?'

She said slowly, 'In principle, I like it very much, although I can see a clash of interest between the ordinary guests, as it were, and those from the company. I suppose the thing to do would be to have certain rooms free at all times.' She paused, then said with constraint, 'But of course, this is really none of my business.'

'On the contrary.' Lyall was smiling now. 'A major factor in making the place a success will be having an experienced manageress—someone who knows how to put edgy people at ease. I'd like to offer you the job, Mrs Pentreath, and I hope very much that you'll consider it.'

'She'll do nothing of the sort!' Morgana was on her feet. 'I think it's an insult—to offer my mother a job in her old home!'

'An insult was the last thing I intended, believe me.' He was still watching Mrs Pentreath. 'It seemed to be a solution to both our problems. Was I wrong to suggest it?'

'Why, no.' Elizabeth drew a long quivering breath. 'You've just taken me by surprise a little, that's all. May I have time to think about it?'

'As long as you wish.'

'She doesn't need time,' Morgana declared passionately. 'And she doesn't need your charity either.'

'I wasn't aware I was offering charity. It's a job for which a salary will be paid.' Lyall sounded slightly bored. 'In addition, your mother will qualify for one of the Corporation's pension schemes, and other benefits.'

'Benefits!' Morgana was almost crying with rage. 'To be a servant in her own home?'

'And what else has she been, ever since this place became a hotel?' he asked coolly. 'You may have been able to kid yourself you were still Miss Pentreath of Polzion, but it's an even bet that your mother's view of the situation was rather more realistic.' He turned back to Elizabeth. 'As I said, I'd like you to think about it. Please ask me any questions you think relevant.'

'Thank you.' She gave a shaky smile. 'I'm sure there will be dozens of things I'll want to know, but for the moment I can't think of one of them.'

'Mother!' Morgana's eyes were fixed on her in a kind of agony. 'You aren't seriously going to consider taking this job, surely?'

'I most certainly am,' said Mrs Pentreath with a kind of robust firmness. 'I'd be a fool not to, darling. After all, where am I going to get a better offer? Now, if you'll excuse me, I'll go and give Elsa a hand in the kitchen.' She bestowed an impartial, if slightly bemused smile on them both, and departed.

There was a long, taut silence, then Lyall said very quietly, 'Are you going to allow your mother to make up her own mind, or are you going to pressure her with scenes and tantrums?'

Morgana stared at him furiously. 'You seem to take it for granted that when she does decide it will be in your favour.'

'No, hers,' he corrected. 'Try and subdue your prejudice and your resentment against me just for a moment or two, and tell me what alternatives you have to offer. If you left here tomorrow, where would you go and what would you do?'

'I've been looking for work,' she said rather haughtily. 'There are residential posts to be had. It's just a matter of waiting until the right one comes along.'

'Precisely—and who knows how long that might be.' He gave her a level look. 'And it would mean your mother would be uprooted from everything she knows, to take pot luck with strangers in an unfamiliar environment. Is that really what you want for her?'

'No,' she admitted in a low voice. 'But nor do I want her to be beholden to you.'

'Why? Because you don't like me—or because you don't trust me?'

'Both,' she said, lifting her chin defiantly, and he laughed.

'I'm not sure I want your liking, little witch. Liking is such a lukewarm expression of emotion, and trust is something that has to be learned.'

Morgana was silent for a moment, then she asked, 'Why didn't you tell us the truth—why didn't you tell us who you really were yesterday?'

'What difference would it have made? Rich man, poor man, I'm still the heir to your father's estate. And as you made clear just now, the fact that I already have money doesn't make it any more palatable.' Lyall paused. 'And I wanted to find out exactly how the land lay. Besides, there was always the chance that you might have recognised me.'

'Recognised you? Why should I do that?'

He shrugged. 'From the newspapers—magazines. They feature me sometimes.'

'I'm sure they do,' she said sarcastically. 'And not only on the financial pages either.'

He raised his brows. 'Unfortunately I'm not responsible for newspaper editors' sense of priorities. That's another reason why I preferred to keep my identity secret when I first came down here. When the papers get hold of this story, they'll have a field day, and I have a feeling I was spotted by a stringer for one of the dailies in Truro last night.'

'The price of fame,' she jibed.

He gave her a cool look. 'Everything has its price. Morgana. I wonder what yours is.'

'I'm not for sale.' She felt her breathing quicken under his ironic gaze, and knew angrily that he was aware of it too. 'You may be able to buy my mother, but you'll never buy me. I'm not interested in your slick plans for this house, and I shan't be here when they come to fruition.'

'That's a pity,' he said. 'Wouldn't you like to see the house restored to its former glory?'

'Not particularly—and I'm not convinced that that's what will happen, anyway. It'll turn into one of these horribly anonymous plastic palaces that you can find anywhere. You have no real feeling for the place—you can't have. You weren't born here. You haven't loved it all your life.'

'Warts and all?'

'If you want to put it like that,' she said stiffly.

Lyall laughed. 'But witches are supposed to be able to charm away warts. Is that what you do when you look at the house, Morgana? Do you see it with the eyes of enchantment? Others won't, you know. And I have to do something with the place.'

'You could sell it,' she said slowly.

'I could,' he agreed. 'Are you going to make me an offer?'

'Do you think we wouldn't have done if we could have afforded to?' She spoke so passionately, her voice almost broke. 'No—but there is someone else interested—the Donlevens who bought the Home Farm from us.'

'The parents of the gorgeous Elaine?' he queried, and she nodded. He smiled a little. 'I see, but I'm not looking for a purchaser. I think we should keep the place in the family, don't you?'

'What do you know about the family?' she asked fiercely. 'On your own admission you don't even use the family name any more—except when it suits you, of course.'

'Nevertheless it's still the name on my birth certificate, lady, and there isn't anything that can alter that. And don't forget that I come from a long line of black sheep of this particular family, so you can't blame me if that colours my thinking sometimes. I wasn't brought up to have any great love for this house, or any of its occupants, for that matter. Resentment and prejudice aren't your sole prerogative, Miss Pentreath of Polzion. Some of it went across the Atlantic to the United States with my grandfather.'

She shrugged. 'Well, he has his revenge in full now.'

'Indeed yes, if he'd lived to enjoy it.' Lyall paused, then said abruptly, 'Is there anywhere else to have lunch other than the hotel dining room? I want to talk business with your mother, and I don't need an audience.'

Morgana was taken aback. 'Well, sometimes we eat in the kitchen. But there'd be Elsa. She's always been like one of the family, and she does take an interest in everything that happens—sometimes to an embarrassing extent.'

He nodded. 'That's understandable. After all, any decision I take affects her too.'

'Not necessarily,' Morgana said coolly. 'She's a marvellous cook. She wouldn't be out of work for long.'

'I don't intend she shall be out of work at all,' he said, too patiently. 'Why break up a winning team? She'll need help, of course.'

'Perhaps you'd better consult her on that subject,' Morgana said frankly. 'She can be rather—temperamental, and it's reflected in the food sometimes. We—try not to upset her too much.'

'How wise.' Lyall sounded amused. 'Is she upset by my arrival, or do you think lunch will be safe?'

'The fact that she was telling your fortune seems to be a good sign,' Morgana admitted. 'Especially if she saw a future of unmitigated gloom. She has a penchant for alarm and despondency.'

He shook his head. 'She saw wealth and an eventful love life. Who could ask for more?'

In her mind's eye, Morgana could see the spread of cards across the table dominated by the Queen of Hearts in the middle. The Queen of Hearts—Elaine's card.

She said coldly, 'It needn't be foreknowledge, you know. You don't look like a pauper, and you're not exactly the picture of an innocent abroad, either.'

'Well, thank you for those few kind words,' he said sardonically. 'An even simpler explanation would be that Elsa reads the newspapers too.'

Morgana shook her head. 'If she'd recognised you, she would have said something. Elsa isn't good with secrets.' She hesitated. 'I suppose—Mr Trevick knew.'

'Not until this morning, although I think he had his suspicions.'

'What a pity Elaine recognised you,' she said. 'You could have gone on with your little joke almost indefinitely. Is—is she a great friend of this—Lindsay van Guisen?'

'My stepsister,' Lyall supplied smoothly. 'I wouldn't know. Lindsay has a wide and ever-increasing circle of friends, and she enjoys giving parties. You don't have to have a close and intimate relationship to get invited. Why do you ask? Would you like to go to one of them?'

'Oh, no,' she said hastily. 'Out of my league altogether. I—I was just curious, that's all. Besides, you've been asking questions about us and our lives. I think I'm entitled to know a little about yours in return.'

'Ask what you want.'

'Well, are there any more little secrets you're keeping from us? Like a wife and fifteen children, for example.'

'I'm certainly not married,' he said drily. 'And I've never been notified of the existence of any children. Does that satisfy you?'

'It's a matter of complete indifference to me if you run a harem,' she said sharply. 'What I'm trying to say is that from now on I'd prefer you to be honest with us.'

'Starting from now?' He glanced at her quizzically.

'Yes,' she nodded. 'You see, I really don't trust you, Mr Lyall Pentreath van Guisen. You're a business man, not a philanthropist, and the way you've created this job for my mother—made her an offer she can't refuse—is altogether too smooth, too well thought out. There must be a hidden snag you haven't mentioned yet.'

'Clever girl,' he approved. 'Or was it just a lucky guess?'

She stared at him. 'You admit it?'

'Naturally,' he said. 'Total honesty you wanted. Total honesty you shall have.'

'But of course, you're not going to tell me what it is,' she said sarcastically.

'Why not?' He shrugged. 'I'd have had to mention it sooner or later. You see, Morgana, what I'm actually offering your mother is a package deal. I want her to go on running the hotel with the same gentle charm she exerts at the moment. I want Elsa to remain and do the cooking. And I want you.'

'Me?' Her heart began that low, sickening pounding again as she stared at him. 'What for?'

He smiled slowly, his eyes running over her in a way that sent the warm blood pouring into her face.

'I want to take you to bed,' he said gently.

She gasped, pressing her fingers against her heated cheeks. 'How dare you!'

'You said total honesty,' he reminded her almost casually.

'That doesn't give you the right to insult me!' she snapped wildly, her small rounded breasts rising and falling rapidly in her agitation.

'What insult? You asked me a question, lady, and I gave you the answer. It might not have been the one you wanted to hear, but that's just your bad luck. It's the truth, Morgana. I want you and I mean to have you.'

She dug her nails into the palms of her hands, fighting for self-control.

'I've already told you, I'm not for sale.'

'And I'm not buying. What I want from you, you'll give me.'

'You're mad!' She got unsteadily to her feet. 'I refuse to listen to any more of your crude remarks!'

She took a step towards the door, but he moved with all the lithe grace of a jungle animal, blocking her way, his hand moving almost casually to fasten on her arm. Through the wool of her sweater she was conscious of the pressure of his fingers, his touch burning her, as if his hand lay on her naked flesh. She faced him defiantly.

'Let go of me, please.'

'When I'm good and ready,' he clipped in return. 'You're a delectable little autocrat, but I give the orders here now.'

'Not to me,' she denied. 'Never to me. I have no intention of working here—working for you in any capacity whatsoever, and you'd better believe it.'

He said slowly, 'I think you'll change your mind.'

'I know I shan't. Now take your hands off me!'

He grinned, his mouth twisting as he stared down at her. 'You sound almost convincing. That outraged note is quite effective,' he remarked. 'The trouble is I don't want to stop touching you, and if you're honest, you'll admit that isn't what you actually want either.'

'I want you to leave me alone,' she muttered in a savage undertone.

'Stop lying to me.' His own voice deepened, developed a husky note. His eyes held hers for a long moment, then travelled to her parted lips. His proximity, the warmth of his body made every nerve ending tingle in warning. She was suffocatingly aware that the slightest movement on her part would bring their bodies into contact. The blood in her veins seemed to be running slow and heavy, in contrast to the uncontrolled hurry of her breathing, and every pulse in her body had its own separate beat. And she knew that he was quite right. That she didn't want him to stop touching her, but to draw her closer yet, against the lithe hardness of his body, while his mouth took possession of hers unhurriedly, and eternally.

She felt the shock of that realisation penetrate every fibre of her being, then, her face flaming, she tore herself free of his grasp and recoiled from him, almost stumbling over the hearthrug in her haste.

At a safe distance, she faced him again, her chin tilted haughtily.

'I think your past conquests must have gone to your head,' she said coldly. 'But please understand that I haven't the slightest interest in you, either as an employer or a man. And now, if you'll excuse me, I do have other things to do.'

She went towards the door, half expecting him to stop her again, but this time he made no movement at all. At the door, she risked a glance back at him, but he had turned away back towards the fire and was apparently intent on lighting one of the dark cheroots he smoked.

Once safely out of the room, Morgana ran upstairs to her bedroom. She closed the door behind her, and on an impulse turned the key in the lock, something she would normally never have dreamed of doing. Her legs felt oddly weak, and she leaned against the solid panels for a moment or two trying to regain her equilibrium.

She had never in her life been made so aware of her own sexuality, of the vibrant potential of her womanhood, and this unexpected, unwanted self-revelation had shaken her to the core. She lifted her head and stared dazedly across the room into her dressing table mirror, half expecting to see a stranger's face reflected there. Because inwardly she knew she was not the same person who had dressed in that room earlier in the day, or who had stood in front of that mirror, brushing out her cloud of dark hair. She shivered and ran shaking hands over her denim-clad hips, and down the warm, smooth length of her thighs.

Escape was the only answer, she told herself, trying to

be calm and practical. She had not bargained for the fact that physical attraction could outweigh a clash of personalities, amounting to open hostility.

She hated Lyall Pentreath van Guisen, or whatever he chose to call himself, but she could not deny that the touch, the taste of him made her bones melt in the most disturbing manner. Slowly she pushed up the sleeve of her sweater and looked at her arm. The marks of his fingers were still visible, as if he had put a brand on her, the mark of his possession.

Only he doesn't possess me, she thought fiercely, and he never will. I've let him get too close already. It must never happen again, or I could betray myself completely, and if that occurred, then how could I ever live in peace with myself or respect myself ever again?

She took a few slow deep breaths, willing herself back to self-control, determinedly trying to avert her mind from the rather panic-stricken tenor of her thoughts.

He had caught her off her guard, that was all it was, she thought. The grief of her father's death and the subsequent revelations about the entail had left her emotionally vulnerable, and a man as experienced as Lyall obviously was would have had little difficulty in recognising this and turning it to his own advantage. It was the same with everything, she told herself. The job he had offered her mother was a case in point. He had recognised Mrs Pentreath's bewilderment and need for security and used it, gaining in the process not just a manageress for his new project but credit for having made a generous gesture. Because that was how it would undoubtedly be interpreted by their friends and neighbours. It would be said locally that the new owner of Polzion had acted well by Martin Pentreath's widow, and he would have created himself some easy goodwill in the area, as well as incurring Elizabeth's own gratitude.

God, he's despicable, Morgana thought, her hands clenching into fists. He has every angle weighed up in advance. I hate him!

She walked across the room and sank down on to the cushioned window seat. The early promise of the day had faded, and clouds were gathering over the sea. As she watched, the first raindrops dashed themselves against the window, and she shivered again, wrapping her arms tightly round her body. It was painful to sit here, looking at the familiar view and know that it would soon be lost to her for ever. When she returned to Polzion, it would be as a visitor, and she would have to time her visits carefully so that they didn't coincide with Lyall's, she thought, and they would also have to fit in with the demands of her new employer.

She gave a little sigh. She couldn't have chosen a worse time for trying to find a job, she thought bleakly. Apart from the high level of unemployment all over the country, this was now the off-season for hotel work, which was the only thing she was in any way qualified for. She had taken a short commercial course while she was at school, and although her shorthand was a little rusty, her typing was reasonably efficient, and it was this skill she would have to exploit on the open market. It was little enough to offer, she thought ruefully, but the comparative security of her life at Polzion had made any further training seem unnecessary, and if she was honest, she had rather enjoyed being her parents' Girl Friday.

She would drive into Polzion village during the afternoon and buy some papers and magazines so that she could study the situations vacant columns, she decided. There was no time to be lost.

She started slightly as there came a quiet knock on the door.

'Who—who is it?' she called, noticing with annoyance the distinct tremor in her voice.

'It's me, darling.' Mrs Pentreath sounded rather anxious. 'Are you all right? Lunch will be ready soon.'

'Just a minute.' Morgana uncurled herself from the window seat and hurried across the room. Her mother had already tried the door, and was now rattling at it ineffectually, probably under the illusion that it had stuck in some incomprehensible manner.

'You locked it.' Elizabeth Pentreath looked at her daughter in consternation as she came into the room.

'Whatever is the matter?'

'Nothing,' Morgana lied, forcing herself to smile re-
assuringly at her mother. 'I—I have a slight headache,
that's all, and I felt like some peace and quiet.'

'Oh dear!' Mrs Pentreath gave a little sigh. 'Lyall said
he thought he'd upset you, and he has, hasn't he?'

Morgana's lips tightened. 'You could say that,' she ac-
knowledged quietly.

'Darling,' Mrs Pentreath made a little helpless gesture,
'you mustn't take his teasing quite so seriously. You're not
usually so ready to rise to people's bait. I don't understand
your attitude to Lyall.'

'It isn't really so difficult,' Morgana said grimly. 'I don't
like him, that's all.'

'You've made that more than obvious,' her mother
agreed. 'I wish you'd try to be a little more willing to
compromise, darling. It would make life for all of us so
much easier.'

'I doubt that, actually.' Morgana smiled tightly. 'But
I'll try and be civil for my remaining time here.'

'Your remaining time?' Mrs Pentreath stared at her.
'What do you mean?'

Morgana gave a little shrug. 'Well, now that your
future is taken care of, I can start giving my own some
consideration. I need work too, you know.'

'But you have a job here,' her mother protested. 'Didn't
Lyall explain what it was he wanted?'

'Oh, yes,' Morgana said grimly, 'he explained very fully.
Not that it makes the slightest difference. I have no intention of remaining here under his régime, as well he knows.'

'He knows nothing of the sort,' Mrs Pentreath said
roundly. 'On the contrary, he expects you to remain here
and work with me. It's—it's what he calls a package.'

Morgana nodded. 'Yes, I'm aware of that, but I'm not
buying, as I've made more than clear.' She realised her
mother was staring at her oddly and asked resignedly,
'What's the matter, Mother?'

'It's just—you don't seem to understand the situation. I
thought Lyall had told you.'

'Told me what?'

'About the package. He wants everything to go on here exactly as before, with my supervising the housekeeping and you doing the reception work, and providing secretarial services if required.'

'I think that's carrying his charitable impulses rather too far,' Morgana said coldly. 'He must have people working for the van Guisen-Lyall company who are far more highly trained and efficient than I am.'

'I'm sure the same thing applies in my case,' Mrs Pentreath said candidly. 'But the fact is, Morgana, he regards us as a team, and he likes the atmosphere we've achieved in the house. He wants the same—ambience for the new project.'

'Well, you'll supply it for him, love,' said Morgana. 'You're much better at soothing people's ruffled feathers and creating a serene environment than I am.'

'But that's what I'm trying to tell you!' Mrs Pentreath almost wailed. 'He wants us as a team—both of us, or neither of us. I told him I didn't think you'd agree, but he was adamant. And he said that you'd assured him you'd do whatever you had to, because you wanted me to be happy. He said you'd told him you'd do anything to help.'

'My God!' Morgana muttered blankly, and fell silent, remembering her hasty assertion of concern.

Elizabeth Pentreath's mouth trembled. 'It would only be for a year, darling. He promised that. He's having proper contracts drawn up for Leonard Trevick to look at.'

'Then I hope he reads the small print.' Morgana's voice shook, and she turned away.

'Lyall's trying to be kind.' Her mother's voice followed her. 'He's in a difficult position. He feels very strongly that you should have a breathing space here to decide what you want to do. He doesn't think you should do anything hasty so soon after poor Daddy's death.'

'Oh, that's so good of him,' Morgana said savagely. 'And his motives are so pure, naturally.'

'Darling!' Mrs Pentreath shook her head bewilderedly. 'I don't feel I know you when you're like this. Are you implying that Lyall has some ulterior reason for making this offer?'

For a crazy moment, Morgana wondered what would happen if she said baldy, 'He wants to seduce me.' But she couldn't say it. For one thing, it would sound so utterly ridiculous. After all, she was a girl of her own time, not a hysterical Victorian miss who couldn't fend for herself.

She said quietly, 'I wouldn't know what his motives are, but I think it's obvious that he hasn't made this offer out of the goodness of his heart.'

'He is related to us,' Mrs Pentreath observed fairly.

'Very remotely, and I'm sure that old chestnut about blood being thicker than water doesn't apply to him.' Morgana's tone was bitter.

'But he has made the gesture,' Mrs Pentreath persisted. 'It's a wonderful opportunity, for both of us. Surely you can bring yourself to meet him halfway over it? You know how much it would mean to me to be able to stay here. And Lyall won't be here that much, you know. Van Guisen-Lyall is a world-wide corporation. He'll have far more important things to occupy him than us. We probably won't see him for weeks on end.'

Morgana sighed. 'There are other jobs,' she said gently. 'But I do know how much Polzion means to you.'

'It does,' Elizabeth Pentreath said eagerly. 'Won't you try, for my sake?'

Morgana was silent for a tortured moment, while through her mind went all the very cogent reasons why she shouldn't spend a minute longer in Lyall's company than she was forced to. And then she saw her mother's face, suddenly small and vulnerable, her eyes mirroring her anxiety and disappointment, as she waited for her decision.

Impulsively she went to her mother's side and put an arm round her shoulders.

'I'll try,' she said. 'I can't promise more than that, but I will try.'

'Bless you, darling!' Mrs Pentreath smiled mistily. 'You won't regret it, I know.'

'Won't I?' Morgana's tone was ironic. 'I think that

remains to be seen.'

'And you'll come down for lunch now? We're having it
in the kitchen so that Lyall can talk to us.'

Morgana felt frankly as if food would choke her, but
she knew her mother would be upset if she refused to go
downstairs, so she acceded reluctantly and followed her
out of the room.

Lyall was standing in the hall waiting as they came
down the stairs. Morgana avoided looking at him directly,
but she was aware just the same that he was watching her.

As her mother hurried on ahead, to make sure the preparations for the meal were complete, Morgana felt his
hand on her arm. He said softly in her ear, 'My game, I
think.'

She shrugged, still not meeting his gaze. 'But not the
match. And I warn you, I'll fight you at every step.'

She heard him laugh. He said, 'I wouldn't have it any
other way, little witch. It will make the eventual victory
even more satisfying.'

'For one of us,' she said shortly.

His hand shot out, tangling in her hair, bringing her to
halt with a little cry of pain, and forcing her to face him.
Mutinously she stared up at him, loathing his sardonic
smile and the frankly sexual appraisal in his eyes.

'For both of us, Morgan le Fay,' he drawled, and then
she was free, and his long stride was taking him down the
passage to the kitchen, and the delectable aromas which
were seeping round the half-opened door.

Morgana stood quite still, watching him go, wondering
if the note she had heard in his voice had been a warning
or a caress—and why it should matter anyway.

CHAPTER FIVE

IT was one of Elsa's more distinguished meals—the ducklings crisp and succulent, followed by an apple tart with a great bowl of clotted cream—but Morgana only went through the motions of eating and pretended enjoyment.

All her attention was concentrated on Lyall, who sat opposite, watching him charm her mother into unquestioning submission. It made her blood boil, and turned the food to ashes in her mouth.

She was conscious too of Elsa giving him approving glances as she bustled backwards and forwards with the food for the dining room. He was talking about the improvements he was planning for the house, and she knew that what he was saying made a great deal of sense, but that did not lesssen her resentment. It infuriated her to hear him talk of things that had needed doing for years, but for which the money had never been available. She felt she would rather live with the damp that discoloured the wallpaper in the ground-floor rooms and the faulty wiring than submit to what she could only feel was the rape of her home.

'Some of the bedrooms have large built-in cupboards,' he was saying to Elizabeth, who was listening with rapt attention. 'They're really so much wasted space. It would be far better to convert them to shower units. Each room should have some form of washing facility.'

Morgana broke in sarcastically, 'Wouldn't it be easier just to pull the whole house down and start again?'

He didn't even bother to reply, just looked at her wearily and lifted his shoulders in a slight shrug, before continuing his conversation with her mother.

'I'll get Paul Crosbie down,' he said. 'He's a qualified surveyor as well as being one of our advisers. He'll be able to say how far any structural alterations or repairs will have to go. But at the same time it's essential that the character of the place should be preserved.'

'I suppose we must be grateful for small mercies,' Morgana muttered, pushing her uneaten portion of apple tart away from her, to a disapproving cluck from Elsa.

'And I shall be glad to hear any suggestions for improvements that you have,' Lyall went on as if she hadn't spoken. He smiled at Elizabeth. 'I'm sure there are things you'd have liked to have done over the years.'

'Many things,' she said wistfully. 'This kitchen, for instance . . .'

She paused and Elsa broke in indignantly, 'No one's to lay a hand on my range, mind! 'Tes a good old stove and years of life left in it. I know it and it knows me.'

'It's a relationship I heartily approve of,' said Lyall, leaning back in his chair and contemplating his empty plate with satisfaction.

'Would'ee like another morsel of tart?' Elsa wheedled., but he shook his head regretfully.

'I have things to do this afternoon.' He shot a swift glance at Morgana. 'I'd like to see the rest of the house, particularly the attics.'

'Well, I'm sure Morgana would be only too pleased to show them to you,' said Mrs Pentreath without the slightest certainty.

'Is this farce really necessary?' Morgana flared. 'The house is yours. Do you really need a conducted tour?'

'You know its history. I don't,' he gave her a level look. 'Look on it as part of the duties for which I'm paying your salary. That may make it rather less distasteful for you.'

'Nothing will do that,' she said coldly, pushing back her chair and rising. 'Besides, I had other plans for this afternoon.'

'Then they'll have to be postponed or cancelled,' he said. He grinned sardonically as he saw her brows draw together in a swift scowl. 'You could bear in mind that the quicker I see the rest of the house and can make some sort of plan, the sooner I'll be away from here. I do have other things to do. I have to be in Sweden next week.'

'I'm sure we're all duly impressed,' Morgana said bitterly, and walked out of the kitchen. She was halfway along the passage when Lyall caught up with her.

'Pleased with yourself?' he asked drily. 'Feel that you've scored a few points? Your little barbs aren't hurting me at all, lady, but they are upsetting your mother for whom you express such profound concern. I'd like to see some real evidence of it.'

'I'm staying here, aren't I?' she flashed. 'Wasn't that what it was all about? I'm sorry if you don't like my attitude, but it's the only way I know to try and convince you how totally unacceptable you are to me.'

'Try convincing yourself first,' he came back at her, and Morgana gasped, swift colour flooding her face.

'Your conceit is boundless!' she raged.

'And so is your capacity for self-deception.' He sounded weary again. 'Now can we postpone this particular battle to another occasion? I really would like to see those attics.'

'What do you plan for them?' she asked, turning resignedly towards the stairs. 'A sauna and massage parlour?'

'I like your thinking,' he approved gravely. 'But as a matter of fact I was wondering whether they'd convert into a self-contained flat for your mother and yourself.'

'I suppose you're afraid we should intrude upon your guests.' she said coldly.

'On the contrary, my main aim is to provide you with a little privacy—or are you totally devoted to the present arrangement?'

Morgana was tempted to reply 'Yes' stonily, but common sense prevailed.

'It would be better if we had a place of our own,' she admitted. 'My father liked the idea of the guests living *en famille*, but it does get a little wearing at times.'

'At least we can agree on something,' Lyall commented. 'What are the attics used for at the moment?'

She shrugged. 'Not a great deal. We never come up here. There's junk going back for generations. Daddy always meant to sort everything out—but he didn't get around to it,' she added, giving him a challenging glance.

Lyall nodded. 'I imagine the condition of the attics was the least of his problems,' he said drily.

They went up the narrow, uncarpeted secondary staircase which led to the top floor, Lyall bending his head to avoid the low beams and arches of the gabled roof.

'I suspect there's worm in these timbers,' he said.

'I don't doubt it,' Morgana said indifferently. 'Well, here are the attics. The doorway's rather low.'

'You shouldn't have warned me,' he said pleasantly. 'Think of the enjoyment you could have derived from watching me fracture my skull.'

The first room they went into was piled high with dusty furniture. Lyall gave it a cursory glance.

'Infested as well, I expect,' he said. 'The best thing would be to make a bonfire of the lot.'

'You can't do that,' Morgana protested. 'There might be some treasures among it.'

'I think if there were, they'd have found their way downstairs or more probably to the saleroom by now,' he said coolly, eyeing a wicker chair with a broken seat. 'However, if you want to sift through it all, I have no objections.'

She said stiffly, 'You're probably quite right. There's nothing really worth saving.'

'That's quite an admission,' he said mockingly. 'Can I be sure if I organise the appropriate bonfire, that I won't be accused of being an unfeeling vandal?'

She flushed slightly. 'I don't imagine that any accusations I might level would make a great deal of difference, once your mind was made up.'

Lyall inclined his head. 'I'm glad you're beginning to see my point of view.' He stood still, looking around him. 'This room is really quite spacious. Are the others like this?'

'Most of them are. I think the couple at the end are smaller.'

'So they could potentially convert to a kitchen and bathroom,' he said thoughtfully.

She shrugged. 'Now that you mention it, I suppose— yes.' A thought occurred to her. Staring down at the floorboards, and tracing a pattern in the dust with her toe, she said slowly, 'If this conversion goes ahead, just how self-contained and private will it be?' He glanced at her his brows raised interrogatively, and she hurried on. 'I mean, when you come here—or if you do—where would you expect to stay?'

'You sound nervous,' he mocked.

'If I am,' she muttered between her teeth, 'then you have no one but yourself to blame. Frankly, I'm not used to your brand of sexual innuendo.'

'I thought I'd done more than hint,' he said coolly. 'What's the matter, Morgana? Surely you aren't implying you don't know what it is to be desired by a man?'

'I didn't say that,' she protested.

'I'm relieved to hear it,' he said sardonically. 'I wouldn't have liked to think you could have reached your present ripe age, untouched by human hand.'

'I appreciate your concern,' her voice was edged with sarcasm, 'but it's both unnecessary and unwanted. My private life is my own affair.'

'Do all these loaded references to your private life cover Robert Donleven, or is there a string of eager swains queueing for your favours?' he enquired.

'That's got nothing to do with you,' she snapped. 'And how do you know about Rob anyway?'

'I think his name came up in conversation,' he said silkily.

'I bet it did,' she said furiously. 'You really enjoy prying, don't you?'

He shrugged. 'You could put it like that. I prefer to think of it as having all the relevant facts at my disposal.'

'Well, I don't see how Rob comes into that category.'

'Don't you?' He smiled slightly. 'I intend to have his woman. I imagine he'd find that more than relevant.'

Morgana said in a stifled voice, 'I wish you'd stop saying things like that. We—we have to try and get along together somehow, it seems—and I don't find your remarks in the least amusing.'

'Neither do I. In fact, I was never more serious in my life,' he said. His eyes met hers, and their expression made her moisten suddenly dry lips with the tip of her tongue. There was a long, loaded pause, then he added, 'But if it worries you, I can safely say that you and your mother will have this flat to yourselves. Is that what you wanted to hear?'

'Why—yes.' She felt foolish, suddenly.

He smiled slightly and walked on towards the door which communicated with the next attic, and eventually Morgana made herself follow him, to find him standing studying discoloured patches on the plaster above him with a critical stare.

'The roof wants attention,' he commented.

Her lips parted helplessly as she stared at him. She couldn't fathom these sudden changes of mood he seemed to display, the way his attention could switch from stripping her naked with his eyes one minute to the examination of a leaking roof the next.

He didn't, however, appear to notice her silence. 'What are these?' He walked over to a stack of paintings in heavy frames, propped against one wall. 'More family portraits?'

'I don't think so,' she said rather huskily. 'Mostly rather gloomy landscapes and some bad studies of dogs and horses, from what I can remember. I think we kept them for the frames.'

He nodded abstractedly, turning them over. Then he stiffened slightly.

'Mostly, but not all,' he said, gesturing her to his side. 'Meet Grandfather Pentreath—not yours, but mine. I suppose he was banished here after the great rift.'

'I suppose he must have been,' she agreed rather awkwardly, looking down at the thin, arrogant face that stared up at her from the portrait. She said slowly, 'He must have been quite young when this was painted, and when the quarrel took place. He was very good-looking.' she added, realising too late and with dismay that Mark Pentreath had been the image of the tall man who stood at her side. She expected some sardonic remark, but Lyall remained silent, and glancing at him, she realised that there was a slightly bitter twist to the firm mouth.

She said slowly, 'They're so stupid, these family feuds. They begin—and no one has the guts to stop them. I wonder if either of our grandfathers could remember if they were here now, how it all began?'

'I understand it began over a woman,' he said. 'And don't look so surprised. Our generation hasn't a monopoly on sexual passion, although it sometimes gives that impression.'

'It isn't that.' Morgana flushed a little. 'It's—just my memories of Grandfather. He was very old when I knew him, of course, but I always had the idea that he was very upright and moral—and very happily married to my grandmother. I didn't think he would have been the type to have—adventures.'

'In other words, the rakes all come from our side of the family,' said Lyall, faintly amused.

'Well, perhaps.' She lifted a defensive shoulder. 'There's always been a wild streak in the Pentreaths. No one has ever pretended differently.'

'And how does it evidence in you?' He put out a hand and lifted a strand of thick waving hair which hung to her shoulders.

'It doesn't,' she said shortly, resisting an urge to pull away, and trying to ignore the tremor which had possessed her as his fingertips brushed lightly against her earlobe.

'No?' His smile widened. 'Dancing widdershins round standing stones is quite usual for you, is it, Morgan le Fay?'

'Don't call me that,' she said pettishly. 'And I wasn't dancing widder—whatever you call it. I was indulging in a silly superstition. If I'd thought for one minute I was being watched . . .' She paused and gave him a fulminating look.

He grinned mockingly, then bent and lifted the portrait of Mark Pentreath clear of the other dusty frames.

'I think we might restore him to the family gallery,' he remarked. 'Or have you any objection?'

'Why should I? I've already said I think these feuds are silly.'

Lyall propped the picture with a certain amount of care against an ancient chest of drawers. 'Does that mean you want to call a truce between us, Morgana Pentreath?'

'No, it doesn't,' she said coldly, annoyed with herself for having given even a hint of weakness.

'Good,' he said coolly. 'Because I warn you now, only your unconditional surrender will do.' And ignoring her muffled gasp of fury, he walked into the next room.

Morgana was sorely tempted to leave him to continue his tour of the attics alone, and return downstairs, putting her foot through Mark Pentreath's portrait on her way out, but she controlled herself with something of an effort. If she could prove to him, and to herself, that she would not rise to his bait, then life at Polzion might become more tolerable. Like most tormentors, she thought, Lyall would soon tire of a victim who made no response to his goading.

She pinned on a cool smile and followed him.

'I'm sorry for all the mess,' she apologised sweetly. 'You won't find any missing portraits in here, just a lot of old clothes and things.'

'So I see.' Lyall glanced around, his brows raised. 'Did anyone in this family ever throw anything away.'

'Why, yes.' She hesitated. 'Actually, nearly all these things belonged to my grandmother. When she died, Grandfather moved everything up here—her clothes, letters, photographs. I imagine he planned to go through it all eventually, but he never did. Apparently once or twice he tried, but found it too painful.' She swallowed, memory carrying her back to early childhood and a magical afternoon spent alone up here going through the trunks, unbeknownst to anyone, and finding a dress with floating gauzy skirts in layers like the pointed petals of a flower, and a pair of high-heeled silver shoes. She'd dressed up in them and made her way slowly and carefully downstairs. After all, she was Grandfather's little princess—he was always telling her so—and now she was dressed like a princess.

Even now, she could remember the shock of his violent reaction, the way his eyes had blazed as he struggled to rise from the chair to which his arthritis had confined him eventually.

'Take off that dress!' he'd rapped. 'How dare you touch those things! How dare you meddle! You are never to go near them again—do you hear me?'

The child she had been had fled in tears, shattered by
the ruin of her game of make-believe, and presently her
mother had come to find her and comfort her gently, ex-
plaining as simply as she could that remembered grief
sometimes made people behave oddly.

'He loved your grandmother very much and still misses
her,' Elizabeth had explained. 'You gave him a terrible
shock, darling, but he isn't angry with you—not really.
He knows you didn't mean to make him unhappy.' She
hesitated. 'You see, my pet, you do rather look like her,
and that made it so much worse for poor Grandfather.'

The matter had never been referred to again, but
Morgana had never forgotten it, and even after her grandfather's death she had never been tempted to return and
explore the trunks again. They had been declared taboo,
and she was content to abide by that, although at times
she had remembered—and wondered.

Now she said slowly, 'I suppose you think that's very
sentimental.'

'On the contrary, I approve of a certain amount of
sentiment, provided it's properly directed,' Lyall told her.

He opened the lid of one of the trunks, and stood staring
down. 'Good God,' he said blankly. 'Fashion Down the
Ages. If this isn't a moths' pantry, I suppose a theatrical
costumier might be glad of them.'

Morgana grimaced. 'Perhaps—although I must admit
it sounds like desecration.'

'Well, something has to happen to them,' he said impatiently. 'You don't want to wear them yourself, surely?'

She gave a slight strained smile. 'No, I was cured of
that many years ago. I suppose that's why I tend to regard
these trunks—everything that's up here as sacrosanct. But
nothing is—not now.'

'Is that what you'd prefer?' he asked. 'The status quo
endlessly preserved? The house crumbling, the bills piling
up, your guests muttering, and these rooms gathering yet
more dust and cobwebs?'

'No, I suppose not,' she admitted. 'I realise there has to
be progress.'

'Well, that's a start.' He let the lid of the trunk fall shut, and dusted off his hands. 'If you want to sort through these things and extract anything of value—sentimental or otherwise—then do so. I imagine your mother would have been given any jewellery there was.'

'Yes, I think so.' Not that there had been a great deal, she thought, and now there was probably even less. She looked at the trunks and thought of all the memories they contained, all the past happiness and regret, and gave a little shiver as she recalled a vivid image of her grandfather's face, set in lines of bitterness as he'd stared at her as if he could not bear the sight of her . . .

'Cold?' Lyall asked sharply. 'It's like an ice-box up here.'

'No,' she said huskily. 'A grey goose walking over my grave, that's all.'

He said wryly, 'Don't talk of graves, Morgana. You haven't even started to live yet. Now go on downstairs to where it's warm—or warmer, anyway,' he amended with a twist of his lips. 'I'll follow you presently, when I've had a look at the last couple of rooms.'

'From what I remember, they're empty,' she said, not unwilling to depart. 'Apart from the odd spider,' she added with a slight shudder.

'And other livestock, I suspect,' he said. 'I can't figure whether the subdued rustlings I hear are birds in the eaves or mice.'

'Ouch!' Her skin crawled at the thought. 'In that case, I'll gladly leave you to it.' She went out, trying not to hurry, resisting the impulse to turn and see if he was watching her go.

On the stairs, she paused and took a long, steadying breath. The atmosphere up in the attics had been almost claustrophobic, redolent as it had been of the past. And although she hated to admit it, she found being alone with Lyall for any length of time too disturbing for comfort. She wished she could say with truth that he left her cold, that she was totally indifferent to him, either as a potential employer or as a man, but she knew she would be deceiving herself. Although she believed profoundly in mind over matter, she could not gainsay that there was an attraction between them so strong it was almost tangible. His kisses, the slightest touch of his fingers on her skin, were already indelibly printed on her woman's awareness, but this served to increase her resentment of him rather than lessen it.

She could only hope and pray that he was unconscious of the emotional turmoil she had been thrown into, but it didn't seem likely that he was. It was probably all part of a campaign on his part, she thought angrily, the words 'Unconditional surrender' ringing like a knell in her mind. The egotism, the utter conceit of the man! Did he really imagine that he was that irresistible? Probably past experience had given him that impression, she thought sorely. Well, he would learn his mistake. She had no intention of providing him with a little rural amusement, so that he could add another scalp to his belt.

She went into her room and snatched up her brush, applying it to her hair in short angry strokes.

'I will not be just another conquest,' she muttered defiantly, under her breath, then the violent movements of the brush slowed, and it slipped from her fingers, unnoticed to the carpet, as she looked at herself in the mirror, and for the first time faced the poignant question of exactly what kind of relationship she would want from someone like Lyall.

'No,' she thought, 'not "someone like". Lyall himself. What do I want from him?' Her fingers gripped the edge of the dressing table with painful force, and she closed her eyes to shut out the mirrored image with the enormous, shining eyes and vulnerable mouth.

But she couldn't shut out the voice that whispered to her in the depths of her mind, insidiously and insistently. 'What do I want? Why, all the world and half of heaven. And if he loved me . . .'

She clapped a hand over her mouth as if it had uttered the words aloud.

She thought in panic, 'No, it isn't true. I must be mad, even to let myself think these things. I don't mean it.' And then, as if making a private, silent vow, 'I'm not going to let this happen. I won't. I can't.' And then slowly, the final, damning admission was wrung from her in a kind of anguish. 'I dare not.'

She was very quiet for the rest of the afternoon, so much so that her mother asked her anxiously a couple of times if her headache was still bothering her. She moved like an automaton through the various tasks she had to do, while Mrs Pentreath chatted cheerfully about Lyall's plans for the house.

Morgana said yes and no, and nodded or shook her head when she felt the occasion demanded, but she couldn't infuse any kind of reality into the performance she was giving. Her mind was elsewhere, going round and round in circles like a trapped animal, but always returning to that moment of self-revelation in her room, and the terrifying implications which led from it.

Terrifying, because she had always considered herself a rational being, and now it seemed she was far from any kind of reasonable behaviour or reaction. She had a warm, satisfactory relationship with Rob, so why, why this awful temptation to taste the dark delight that Lyall was offering?

It took a conscious physical effort to enter the bedroom which her mother had allocated for his occupation, and check that everything was in order. It was a simple action which by now had become almost automatic, yet Morgana found herself standing in the centre of the room gazing nervously about her as if she had suddenly intruded into an alien landscape.

She was still standing there, when she heard voices in the passage outside and her mother came in with Lyall at her side. She noticed that he was only carrying one moderately sized suitcase, and hoped it meant that he was not contemplating a protracted stay.

'Darling.' Her mother's voice broke gently across her thoughts. 'No towels. What are you thinking of?'

'I'm sorry.' Morgana started almost guiltily. 'I—I'll go and get them now.' She was careful not to look directly at Lyall as she made her escape. She couldn't have borne to see in his eyes that he was quite aware of her inner turmoil and its cause. And she delayed returning to the room with the missing towels until she was sure that he had gone downstairs.

He had already set his mark on the room, she thought, as she put the towels down. There were brushes, and an electric razor in a leather case lying on the dressing table, and a dark blue silk dressing gown had been tossed across the bed. But no pyjamas, she registered without a great deal of surprise. Typical, she supposed, of his general lack of regard for convention. But this half-resentful reflection could not disperse an unwanted but potently disturbing image of Lyall's lean body, warm and naked beneath the rumpled bedcovers. She turned abruptly and left the room.

When she got downstairs it was to be greeted with the welcome news that he had gone out. She could have sagged with relief, but it was important to hide her emotional state from her mother's perception, so she simply murmured, 'Oh.'

'I've been telling Miss Meakins about Lyall's plans,' her mother announced. 'She was most interested, and a little relieved, I think. It wouldn't be easy to find alternative accommodation at this time of year. People are already booking up for Christmas.'

'And will we be doing the same?' In the depths of an armchair, Morgana curled her long, slender legs underneath her.

'I hardly think we'll be ready by then,' Mrs Pentreath admitted. 'There's such a lot to do. Just think, darling, proper central heating, and all those showers. We shan't know ourselves!'

'No,' Morgana said rather wearily. 'That's what I'm afraid of too.'

Mrs Pentreath gave her a quick glance. 'Darling, we can't live in the past. And even——' her voice broke slightly 'even if—your father—had lived, things couldn't go on as they were. We might have lost Polzion altogether.'

'You think we haven't?' Morgana asked quietly. She sighed. 'But I expect that you're right. There had to be

changes, and we could never have afforded them.' She
was silent for a moment. 'Lyall found a portrait of his
grandfather up in one of the attics.'

'Whatever was it doing up there?' Mrs Pentreath
reached for her bag of tapestry work and produced the
canvas she was working on.

'Gathering dust in involuntary exile, I suppose,'
Morgana returned drily. 'Mother, what was the quarrel
about? The original one between Mark Pentreath and
Grandfather?'

Her mother gave a slight shrug. 'I don't know, dear. No
one was ever prepared to discuss it, as you know. I did ask
your father when we were first married, but he said it had
been a triviality that had suddenly blown up out of all
proportion.' She paused. 'But I often wondered—especially when Giles came back, and there was all that trouble.
Of course, he chose a bad time with your grandmother so
very ill, but he wasn't to know that, poor man. It was all
most unfortunate.'

'Especially in view of current developments,' Morgana
said with a touch of irony.

'What a pity we can't see into the future sometimes.'
Mrs Pentreath searched among her skeins of wool for the
colour she wanted. 'Oh, not as Elsa does, but just enough
to make us act—more responsibly at times. If your father
had known then that there would be a son, and that Giles'
boy would eventually inherit the estate, he might have
behaved a little more reasonably.'

'Perhaps, but the Pentreaths as a whole haven't a good
record for reasonable behaviour,' Morgana said flatly.
And I'm as bad as any of them, she thought achingly.
Aloud, she said, 'Could the quarrel have been over a
woman, do you think?'

'A woman?' Mrs Pentreath looked astounded. 'I never
heard such a thing suggested. Whatever gave you the
idea?'

'Lyall did.' Morgana hesitated. 'It would explain why
no one wanted to talk about it, I suppose. After all,
Grandfather and Grandmother were married at the time,
weren't they? If it had been that sort of thing, that would

have been a good reason to hush it all up.'

'Yes.' Mrs Pentreath laid down her tapestry with a slight frown. 'But I can't really believe it, all the same. Your grandfather was a most devoted husband. I've always understood from everyone who knew him that he never looked at another woman after he met your grandmother. And he's the last person one can imagine caught up in some sordid triangle.'

'Yes.' Morgana thought of the fierce old man with the piercing blue eyes whom she had feared more than loved when she was small. It was difficult to imagine even his love for her grandmother having been in any way a softening influence in his life. He had always had his own brand of arrogance, and a certain amount of moral rectitude that commanded respect, if it could not instil affection. She asked rather abruptly, 'Did Lyall tell you what he plans for the attics?'

'Yes, he did. It all sounds most exciting, and all that space is just going to waste at the moment.'

'Did you know that all Grandmother's things were still up there?'

'I suppose they must be.' Mrs Pentreath digested that for a moment or two. 'Of course your grandfather would never allow them to be touched in any way.'

'As I found out to my cost,' Morgana said rather drily.

'Oh dear, I'd almost forgotten that awful day.' Mrs Pentreath gave a little sigh. 'I couldn't say so at the time, naturally, but I thought it was a great deal of fuss. Children all love dressing up, and a trunkful of old clothes is a natural magnet. And it wasn't as if you'd torn or damaged anything.'

'I thought you were on his side.'

'Let's say I could understand why he reacted as he did, although I couldn't condone it.' Mrs Pentreath threaded her needle with some care. 'He was the master of the house still, and his word was law and always had been. My—position wasn't always as easy as it could have been.'

No, Morgana thought, giving her mother a sympathetic glance. Elizabeth Pentreath's early years in this house must have been fraught with difficulties. Perhaps her husband's subsequent spoiling had been an attempt to make up for this, and for the unexpected career of hotelier's wife which had been thrust upon her, and for which she must have been totally unprepared. Yet, in her gentle, rather harum-scarum way, she had made a success of things as far as she was able. If the business side of it had always been a struggle, she had an innate ability to make people comfortable, and soothe them out of ill-humour into a more mellow attitude to life. It was a gift, and as such it had been recognised by Lyall.

She began to consider for the first time that with a regular salary, and her most pressing financial problems safely shifted to someone else's shoulders, her mother might be able to achieve a degree of happiness and independence which had never been available to her before. No longer shadowed by her husband's extrovert personality, she would be able to develop her own quiet strengths.

Well, Morgana thought grimly, it's an ill wind that blows no good to anyone, and I have to be happy for her.

But in her own life, the wind of change had risen to gale force, and she felt as helpless and vulnerable as one of the drifting leaves in the garden. Suddenly, almost in the passing of a day, self-doubt had become her only certainty, and she was terrified by the violence of emotions whose existence she had never even suspected before.

She looked round at the familiar shabbiness of the room, seeking a reassurance which was denied her. Soon that too would change.

She thought in swift panic, 'Nothing will ever be the same again.' And on the heels of that realisation came another, even more traumatic. 'I shall never be the same again.'

Huddled in her chair, watching the flames licking round the logs on the fire, she tried to rekindle her hate for the man who had turned her world upside down. Tried, and with a kind of despair, failed.

CHAPTER SIX

LYALL did not return that afternoon, and later there came a telephone call to say he would not be back for dinner either. He did not venture any explanation, and Morgana, who took the message, returned the receiver to the rest with a slight thump.

'Treating the place like a hotel!' she muttered crossly, as she went back to her self-imposed task of laying the dinner table, and was forced to smile ruefully as the idiocy of her own remark came home to her.

As the evening wore on, she found she was increasingly on edge, waiting for the sound of his car returning. Ostensibly she was re-reading *David Copperfield*, but for once, young David's trials and tribulations with his step-father Mr Murdstone had no power to hold her attention.

And when the door did open to admit a masculine figure, it was Major Lawson who had been up to London for the day. Morgana found she was looking at his tall, unthreatening figure with real pleasure and relief.

'It's a cold evening,' he said, as he came forward to the fire. 'I wouldn't be surprised if we were to have a frost.'

'Oh dear!' Elizabeth rose from her chair and began to make up the fire. 'Perhaps Elsa is right. She's been saying for weeks that we were going to have a hard winter.'

Major Lawson laughed, the quiet, cool lines of his face dissolving into humour. 'Elsa's prophecies are a joy and a delight, although I must admit I didn't have a great deal of faith in them before today. But when I came here she told me I had a lucky face, and the news I was given today seems to confirm that.'

Elizabeth asked in her gentle voice, 'Has something happened?'

'Something rather startling. I hope it will turn out to be pleasant.' He paused, then said, 'My appointment today was with my agent. Apparently a publisher's bought my novel.'

Morgana gasped, and Mrs Pentreath, said 'Good heavens,' rather helplessly.

'That was rather my own reaction,' he admitted, sitting down on the sofa.

'What kind of a novel is it?' Morgana asked. 'Have you written a great many? I mean——' she hesitated '—should we have heard of you?'

'I wouldn't think so.' He sounded amused. 'It's my first book, actually, and it's a thriller. I'm engaged with the second one at the moment. That's what all the typing is about.'

'Well, we did wonder,' said Morgana, returning his smile. 'It's wonderful news for you.'

'I suppose it is. My feelings are rather mixed at the moment. I can see certain unavoidable changes in my peaceful existence.'

'Oh.' Elizabeth looked at him quickly. 'Does it mean you'll be leaving us?'

'No, certainly not,' he said very positively. 'But my agent warned me that there might be a certain amount of attendant publicity which could be rather trying.'

'I think publicity is something we're all going to have to get used to.' Morgana said resignedly. At his inter-rogative glance, she went on, 'We discovered today that the new owner of this house is the head of some enormous corporation called van Guisen-Lyall.'

'Good God!' Major Lawson leaned forward. 'They really are giants. Had you no idea?'

'None at all,' said Elizabeth. 'I don't really understand the connection fully, although Lyall did try to explain it to me. It seems his mother was a Lyall, and after poor Giles' death—I gather the marriage wasn't a great success—she married one of the van Guisens—the man she'd been intended to marry all along. Lyall and his stepsister inherited everything.'

Morgana wondered when her mother had acquired all this information. She obviously thought from the sympathetic way in which she spoke that she was in Lyall's confidence.

But that, Morgana thought with irony, is a confidence

trick. Oh, Mother, if you only knew! She sat in her chair, staring at the book on her lap, trying to make sense of the meaningless printed symbols on the page, while her mother talked of Lyall and his plans for Polzion, and Major Lawson responded with more information about van Guisen-Lyall. It seemed he had shares in one of their companies, and Morgana found she was listening to what he had to say with increasing alarm. The corporation was infinitely more powerful and complex than she had ever suspected, with ramifications in all sorts of areas—property, engineering, and oil. She realised that one of the things which attracted her to Lyall as well as frightened her was the sense of power which emanated from him—not merely sexual power, but something more dangerous and material. She supposed he was what people called 'a tycoon'. It was a word she had never liked, or understood, and she saw no great reason to change her opinion.

Everything that Major Lawson was saying simply helped to emphasise the unbridgeable gulf that yawned between herself and Lyall. Not that he had any intention of attempting to build a permanent bridge. She had no delusions about that. She would be an interlude, a diversion while he was in Cornwall, far from the hub of everything which made up his world. But when the conversion of Polzion was complete, he would go back to that world—to the boardrooms, and the penthouses, and the VIP lounges at airports. There was no place for her there. On the other hand, to give Lyall credit, he had not indicated that there would be.

She was glad when the conversation switched back to Major Lawson's novel. It was pleasant to sit and watch her mother, her face alight with interest and enthusiasm, and it occurred to her almost idly that Major Lawson must think so too. He included Morgana in his remarks, but only she was sure, out of courtesy. It seemed right that he should be confiding in Elizabeth. People did, and always had, and he was alone. A long time ago, she remembered, he had told her mother he was a widower. Probably they were the nearest thing to a family that he had now. Certainly he preferred to spend his evenings in here, reading or doing a crossword puzzle, rather than go along to the smaller room just off the dining room where the television was, and where Miss Meakins usually spent most of her time.

Eventually Morgana gave up all pretence of reading or listening, and excused herself, bending to kiss her mother goodnight. It was late, and she felt physically and emotionally battered by the events of the past twenty-four hours. But when she got into bed, sleep was elusive, and she lay there staring into the darkness, listening as the grandfather clock in the hall below chimed the quarters and finally the hour of midnight, wondering where Lyall was, and despising herself for wondering.

She finally drifted off to sleep, still listening in vain for the sound of the car, and dreamed she still searched for him through endless rooms where a party was going on, and every other guest was a stranger to her, except one—Elaine Donleven, smiling triumphantly and dressed as the Queen of Hearts.

She felt unrested and at odds with herself when she awoke the following morning, and not even the sight of the garden, sparkling under the cloak of the promised frost, had the power to lift her spirits. The fact that she had overslept didn't help either, and she had to wash quickly, fling on jeans and a sweater and drag a comb through her thick cloud of hair.

Her mother and Elsa were already busy serving the guests' breakfast when she entered the kitchen with a muttered apology, and Morgana lifted the rack of fresh toast and the coffee pot and took it through to the dining room. It was almost a shock to see Lyall there, sitting alone at a small table by the window. A glance at the long dining table where the others sat showed that the toast and coffee was for him, that they were already well supplied, and she had to make herself walk over to where he was sitting and set the food down.

'Good morning.' He folded the paper he was reading—the business section, she noticed—and set it down.

'Good morning,' Morgana responded with equal formality. He had finished his grapefruit and as she reached to pick up the dish with the discarded skin, his fingers closed round her wrist.

'Don't rush off,' he said softly. 'Sit down and have some coffee with me.'

'No, thanks,' she said curtly. 'I do have things to do this morning.'

He shrugged. 'So do I. I was merely suggesting a civilised interlude before we begin.'

She was horribly aware of Miss Meakins' inquisitive gaze devouring the little scene from the adjoining table, and she tugged herself free of his grasp with heightened colour.

'I'm afraid I don't have time for interludes, civilised or otherwise,' she said between her teeth. 'You'll have to excuse me, please.'

His eyes narrowed slightly. 'You look as if you need a break of some kind. You're so tense you might be strung up on wires. What's the matter? Didn't you sleep well last night?'

'Like a log,' she snapped, for the benefit of the avidly listening ears near by. 'I hope you spent a comfortable night.'

'I could think of ways it could have been improved on.' Lyall stretched out a hand for the toast rack and the dish of Elsa's home made marmalade.

'I'm so sorry,' she said insincerely. 'You'd better have a word with my mother. I'm sure she'll be able to put things right.'

'I doubt that.' He spread the marmalade on the toast. 'In any event, I think I shall just let things take their course.' The smile he turned on her was silky, but little devils danced in his eyes, disconcerting her completely. Her flush deepening, she picked up the grapefruit dish and started for the door.

As she went through the hall, the telephone began to ring. She lifted the receiver and heard Rob's voice speaking to her.

Her mind was so filled with Lyall that she responded to his initial greetings almost at random, until she heard his voice sharpen, asking if she was all right.

'Yes—yes, of course I am.' She was instantly remorseful. 'It—it's a wonderful morning, isn't it? Did you want something special?'

'I thought you might like to know the new horse has arrived.'

Morgana gasped. 'Oh, that's great. How is he settling?'

'It's a little too soon to know,' he said, but his tone conveyed a serene satisfaction and conviction that all would be well. 'He looks terrific, and he seems to have a good temperament as well. Even my mother and father are impressed. Can you manage to get over for an hour? I'd love to show him to you.'

'Now that's an invitation I can't refuse,' she said happily. 'Do I get to ride him too?'

'Perhaps, if you make it worth my while,' said Rob with a sinister chuckle.

'Hm, I shall have to think about that,' she teased. 'Perhaps I'll just hire him for an hour later on instead.'

'I don't know whether Elaine is going to be able to bear him to be used for the school.'

'But I thought that was why you'd bought him,' she protested. 'To take the place of Checkmate.'

'Well, that was the intention,' Rob admitted. 'But Elaine seems to have other ideas now that he's actually here. She's always wanted to try some eventing, as you know.'

'You think he could be that good?'

'She thinks so,' he corrected. 'But understandably she doesn't want our usual range of heavy-handed novices ruining his mouth.'

'No, I suppose not,' agreed Morgana, thinking all the same that it was typical of Elaine to acquire a new mount ostensibly for the riding school, and then change her mind and decide the horse was too good for the pupils. And the stables badly needed a good, even-tempered hack. The chestnut gelding Checkmate, which had been their last acquisition, looked mild enough, but proved to have a streak of mischief bordering on absolute malice. He bit, he kicked, he shied, and at the slightest sign of hesitancy on the part of his rider, he bucked. But he was showy to look at and a good jumper, so Elaine rode him in jumping events at gymkhanas and used him as an advertisement for the school.

Morgana said goodbye to Rob, promising she would be over as soon as she was free. As she went back to the kitchen, she realised ruefully that her motive was double-edged. She wanted to see the new horse, about which she had heard so much, but at the same time it was providing her with a cast-iron excuse for getting out of the house.

And when, deliberately casual, she mentioned it to her mother, it was clear Mrs Pentreath had thought exactly the same thing.

'But, darling,' she looked at Morgana, her brows raised, 'Lyall might need you for something.'

Morgana shrugged. 'I hardly think so. We finished the tour of the house yesterday. And I don't intend to live in his pocket. I do have my own life to live.'

'Yes, of course,' Mrs Pentreath agreed. 'But he is our employer now, you know. Perhaps we should consult him about our time off.'

'And perhaps we shouldn't,' Morgana snapped. 'We haven't signed anything yet. He doesn't own us body and soul, and he never will as far as I'm concerned.

'Hoity-toity,' Elsa remarked tartly, coming in from the courtyard. 'Who got out of her bed the wrong side, then?'

'Oh, for heaven's sake!' Morgana exploded. She went to the broom cupboard in the passage and retrieved the Hoover and the dusters and polish, deciding she might as well vent her spleen on the bedrooms. She had always found the physical energy she needed to expand on housework had a profoundly soothing effect, but this morning as she vacuumed and rubbed, her panacea didn't seem to be working. She paid Lyall's room the most cursory of visits, not in the least mollified to find it tidy, with the bed neatly made. But at least it wasn't occupied, she thought, as she unplugged the Hoover. She had that much to be thankful for.

She put her cleaning implements away, and, sticking her head round the office door, told her mother with faint defiance that she was going down to the Home Farm.

'I'll be back in time to help serve lunch,' she added the assurance.

'That's all right, dear.' Elizabeth's eyes were fixed on the column of figures she was adding. 'Lyall's waiting for you. He said he'd give you a lift.'

'How very obliging of him,' Morgana said coldly. 'However, I think I can manage to get there under my own steam.'

Her mother sighed. 'Just as you wish, of course, but I ought to warn you the car isn't behaving too well at the moment. I think it's the battery.'

'Then I'll walk,' Morgana said firmly. She ran up to her room to get her coat, and a scarf for her hair. She was humming a little tune, but it died on her lips when she pushed open her bedroom door and saw Lyall sitting on the window seat.

'What are you doing here?' she demanded angrily.

'Waiting for you.' He rose to his feet unhurriedly. 'It occurred to me that you'd be up to make yourself glamorous for the faithful swain. I was afraid if I hung around downstairs, I might miss you.' It was smoothly said, but she did not miss the glint in his eyes, indicating that he had already accurately gauged her likely reaction to his offer.

'Thank you,' she returned ironically. 'But there was no need to take all this trouble. I can get to Home Farm by myself. And I wouldn't want to take you out of your way.'

'You're not,' he said coolly. 'I'm going there too.'

'You are?' she said weakly, aware that the wind had vanished from her sails yet again.

'I decided to take the lovely Elaine up on her offer of dinner last night, or rather I offered her an alternative,' he told her. 'We ate at a place called the Carte Blanche. Do you know it?'

'I've heard of it,' she replied rather huskily. So that was where he had been—taking Elaine Donleven out to dinner. She supposed she shouldn't really be surprised. Elaine had signalled her intentions quite clearly, earlier in the day, as Lyall had been quick to appreciate. 'You— you don't let the grass grow under your feet, do you?'

'No,' he said. 'I can't afford to. And as I've tried to explain, my time here has to be strictly limited.'

'And you're going over to Home Farm this morning— to see Elaine?'

'She offered to show me the stables,' he nodded. 'I'd be

interested to see them. She seems to have her head screwed on the right way, as well as other assets.'

'Oh, she has,' Morgana agreed. 'Are you interested in horses?'

He shrugged. 'Reasonably so. My stepfather used to keep them on his estate in New Hampshire, but I never had a great deal of time for riding.'

'My God!' Morgana raised her eyebrows. 'Have we actually discovered something at last that the famous Lyall van Guisen doesn't excel at?'

'Perhaps I was too busy perfecting my expertise in other directions,' he said mockingly. 'Would you like a demonstration?' he added, glancing towards the bed.

'Thanks, but no, thanks,' she said unevenly. 'Now will you please get out of my room.'

'If I must. I have seen a woman comb her hair and put lipstick on before.'

'I might be going to change my clothes,' she said defiantly.

'To go riding?' His eyes surveyed the slender length of her jeans-clad legs. 'I don't think so. In either event, I'd prefer to stay,' he added wickedly, watching the instant colour rise in her face.

'To hell with you and your preferences!' she flared. 'I would simply like a little privacy.'

'You've got five minutes,' he told her. 'Elaine has already been on the phone once wanting to know where we are.'

'Where you are, perhaps,' she said coldly. 'I doubt whether my whereabouts are of any great importance to her.'

'I doubt it too,' he said softly. 'But it's not her you're going to see. Unless I miss my guess, it's her brother.'

'That hardly took a great deal of working out,' she said shortly, going across to the wardrobe and jerking open the door. She soon found what she was looking for—a hacking jacket in a warm wool tweed which had seen better days. Uncaring of what Lyall might think, she thrust her arms into the sleeves. It didn't matter what she looked like, she told herself defiantly. She was no competition for Elaine and never had been, so she wasn't going to make a fool of herself by trying at this late stage. She took a silk square from her dressing table drawer and tied it over her hair.

Then she faced him. 'I'm ready.'

He inclined his head courteously, but made no comment. As she went past him, out of the door he was holding open for her, Morgana thought wryly that if he was accustomed to prolonged prinking sessions from the women in his life, the last few minutes must have been a bit of an eye-opener for him. She could imagine, for instance, the amount of time that Elaine would spend before presenting her immaculately groomed self to the world, and she tried to visualise herself in similar circumstances, but failed. She had never had a great deal of time to spend on her appearance, let alone the inclination. And she certainly couldn't afford a lot of expensive cosmetics to pamper herself with. She was fortunate in possessing a clear white skin which needed little assistance, and large eyes heavily fringed with dark lashes. She was slim, without needing to diet, and reasonably attractive, she thought judiciously, but no heads were going to turn when she walked into a room.

'I brought the car round to the front,' Lyall told her when they got downstairs. He opened the front door and ushered her past him.

'I can see that,' she said rather faintly. 'Are you sure Cornish roads are ready for this?'

He lifted a shoulder. 'I make out. Do you want to drive?'

'No!' The thought of trying to control all the latent power concealed in that low-slung, streamlined silver-grey body turned her knees to jelly.

'It's no more dangerous than a broomstick.' He was laughing at her again, reminding her of the embarrassment of their first meeting, and she gave him a stony stare.

'I'm not used to cars that look as if they should be taking part in some Grand Prix,' she said with a lift of her shoulder. 'I prefer my motoring to be rather more sedate.'

'Sedate,' he said, 'is not the word I would normally have associated with you.'

'But then,' she said. 'You don't really know me, do you?

You've just made some hasty assumptions, and now you expect me to fit in with them.'

'I think maybe we won't discuss my expectations of you,' he said softly. 'They only seem to upset you.'

She was about to reply off the top of her voice that there was no way in which he could upset her, but the denial would be so patently untrue and ridiculous that she decided silence might be more prudent.

She subsided into the depths of the passenger seat, staring at the rows of dials and switches on the dashboard, and thanking heaven that bravado hadn't prompted her to take up his challenge and offer to drive the thing.

As he got in beside her, he asked, 'What are you smiling at?'

'I was just thinking,' she said. 'The day you came, I thought perhaps you might have taken a wrong turning and driven straight over the cliff instead. But in this car it probably wouldn't matter. I daresay there's a button you can press which turns it into a jet aircraft, like a souped-up Chitty Chitty Bang Bang.'

'I wouldn't count on it,' Lyall said drily. 'But let's not test it by taking any wrong turnings on our way to Home Farm.'

He drove well. Morgana had to admit that to herself, albeit unwillingly. There was no chance that the large animal that seemed to purr so menacingly under the bonnet was going to run away with them. She watched his hands on the wheel, the long fingers, the well-kept nails, and remembered their touch on her skin. The same control, the same expertise, she thought, and resisted an urge to pull her jacket further round her body.

When they reached the Home Farm, under her directions, Lyall drove under the archway and through the big yard to the stable block at the back. Rob came hurrying to meet them, his smile for Morgana warmly protective. 'Hello, love. Morning van Guisen.'

Lyall got out of the car and stood looking around him. He would find nothing to criticise here, Morgana thought sharply, no scope for conversion or improvement. The buildings were in good order, neatly painted, and the yard clean

and uncluttered. The stables looked both cared for and pros-
perous, and she was glad for Rob's sake that this was so.

Lyall was asking questions, of course, but this was
understandable. He was a businessman, after all, even if
he wasn't very knowledgeable about horses. And he
seemed genuinely interested in the cost of feed and the
other overheads which Rob was responding about.

'I hope you aren't thinking of starting a rival organisa-
tion up at Polzion,' Rob joked, but it was only half a joke,
because even in the summer there wouldn't be enough
people wanting riding lessons or a day's hacking round
the moor and lanes to justify two stables in the area.

Lyall shook his head. 'On the contrary, I was considering whether ultimately I couldn't put some further business your way.' He turned to Morgana. 'Did your father
never think of joining forces with the stables and offering
riding holidays on special terms?'

'No, he didn't,' she said with something of a snap. He
knew as well as she did that Martin Pentreath had been
strictly in the amateur league as a hotelier, and that such a
potentially commercial idea would never have occurred to
him. But it wasn't a thing she particularly wanted to admit.

Rob said with a slight lift in his voice, 'But I like the
sound of the idea. Perhaps we could discuss it some time.'

'Why not?' Lyall agreed. 'I shall be in the area on and
off for the next few months.'

Oh, would he? Morgana thought, smouldering. That
wasn't the impression he'd given previously. What had
happened to the whizz-kid tycoon, jetting all over the
world?

And then Elaine arrived, looking like a glossy advertisement for the latest in riding gear, and Lyall turned to
greet her, a smile curving his mouth, and Morgana realised
that he might have a very potent reason for wishing to
remain in the neighbourhood for longer than he had originally planned.

There was no edge to the way he was looking at Elaine,
just frank male appreciation for an extraordinarily attractive girl. Which she was, Morgana thought, forcing herself
to be fair. The trouble was she knew it too.

She watched Elaine responding to Lyall's greeting now, like an exotic flower opening its petals to the sun. It was a come-on, no one could be in the least doubt of that, but subtly, gracefully done, in a way best designed to flatter a man.

Morgana discovered with a sense of shock that her nails were digging painfully into the palms of her hands. What was the matter with her? she apostrophised herself slightly. It would be an ideal solution for Lyall to become involved with Elaine. She belonged to his world. She even went to the same parties. She was no village maiden to be swept off her feet by the rich rake from the big city. Any affair between them would be conducted on terms they both recognised and accepted.

And I, she thought, would be off the hook. If he was fully occupied with Elaine, then he certainly wouldn't bother with me, and I could relax a little and get on with my life without having to worry about this cat-and-mouse game he's been playing with me.

She should have been elated at the thought, or at least overcome with relief, but there was only a kind of cold emptiness, interspersed with a pain that was almost physical as Elaine put her hand caressingly on Lyall's arm smiled up in his face.

Morgana thought in agony, 'My God, this is jealousy: But it can't be. I can't allow it to be, because that would imply all sorts of other things as well, and I'm not ready for that.'

Dimly she could hear Elaine murmuring something about 'terribly flattered' and Lyall's voice, pitched low with that warm, sensuous note in it. 'I couldn't keep away.'

She wanted to say something loud and ugly like, 'That must have been some dinner party last night,' but instead she bit the soft inner part of her lip until she could taste her blood. Something terrible was happening to her, was threatening to take her over—something she couldn't control, yet she had to, because otherwise she would be on a path to total self-destruction.

Rob said in her ear, 'A penny for your thoughts.'

'Oh, they're worth far more than that,' she tried to speak lightly.

He smiled. 'I bet they are! But at least you still have your old home to live in. He was telling my parents something of his plans for the place last night, while he was waiting for Elaine.'

She said, 'It won't be our old home for very much longer. It will soon just be the place where we happen to work. By the time he's finished with it, I doubt whether it will be recognisable as Polzion. In any event, I have no intention of hanging around to find out. He wants me to remain for the first year, and I will, to make sure my mother is settled and content, and then I shall go. Who knows, I might even train for something, if it's not too late.'

'Of course it isn't too late.' Rob's face was suddenly serious. 'You're barely more than a child, my sweet.' He hesitated. 'Morgana, you don't have to go anywhere. You know that, don't you? I haven't said anything because I felt it was too soon after your father's death, but . . .'

'It is too soon,' she said gently. 'But thank you, Rob. Now, are we going to look at this horse?'

There was plenty to admire when Bartram's Babe was led out of his stall. He was a tall bay gelding, with powerful quarters, and Morgana whistled as she looked at him.

'You utter beauty!' she exclaimed rapturously. 'Rob, have you got some apple?'

Rob supplied the necessary titbit, and Bartram's Babe accepted with delicacy and nuzzled her fingers, blowing on them gently and coaxingly.

'You're a perfect gentleman,' Morgana told him, lovingly, running her fingers down the long, intelligent head. She had been going to add, 'Unlike some I could mention,' meaning Checkmate, but she stopped herself, because a remark like that under the circumstances could be misunderstood, and besides, the germ of an idea had flashed into her mind.

She looked at Rob, smiling brightly. 'And how's Checkmate? I hope his handsome nose hasn't been put out of joint by the newcomer.'

'Oh, he's surviving,' Rob said drily. They walked over to the loosebox where Checkmate was waiting. He looked utterly docile, but Morgana made no offers of apple. 'Carnivore!' she muttered under her breath, as she clicked her tongue lovingly and hypocritically at him, and Checkmate's velvet eyes looked back at her with the expression of a horse in whose mouth butter would have difficulty in melting.

'Another handsome animal,' Lyall remarked, coming up behind them. Morgana looked swiftly at Rob who, she knew, was about to say in cheerful condemnation, 'Oh, he looks all right,' and then go on to list Checkmate's vices, and before he could utter she gave him a hard but unobtrusive kick on the ankle. He gave her a look of pained astonishment, but took the hint. When Lyall had moved away again to speak to Elaine, who was still worshipping at the shrine of Bartram's Babe, he hissed, 'What's up?'

'He might be—on Checkmate,' Morgana whispered back.

'No!' Rob said sharply, and she put a hand on his arm, looking up at him limpidly.

'Oh, Rob, what harm would it do? We could go in the paddock, so that at least he'd have grass to fall on. And only this morning he was talking to me about his horsemanship,' she added, crossing her fingers surreptitiously in her jacket pockets. After all, she argued with herself, it wasn't really a lie. Lyall had been talking about horses. All she'd done was place a rather different interpretation on the conversation. 'Let's see how good he is. After all, Elaine always said Checkmate could sort out the men from the boys.'

'I hope this isn't some hare-brained scheme to try and get him to break his neck,' Rob said glumly. 'I haven't forgotten your lunatic comments about him falling over the cliff.'

'No, of course not,' she said impatiently. 'I'd just like to see a little mud on those immaculate clothes. Ever since he arrived at Polzion, he's been calling all the shots, and I'd love to see him make a fool of himself, just once.'

'Elaine would never allow it,' Rob said flatly.

Morgana shrugged. 'Does she have to know? If she went to make some coffee, we could have a saddle on Checkmate in no time at all. I'd help.'

Rob gave her a caustic look. 'Greater hate hath no woman,' he observed. 'All right—you win, and if he's injured, you'd better pray our insurance will cover it. I don't know what the going rate in millionaires is these days.'

As if Fate was taking a hand, Mrs Donleven walked into the yard.

'Oh, there you are, darling,' she said to Elaine. 'The Templeton girl has phoned. Something about a party, and she seems to think you know all about it.'

'Yes, I do,' Elaine admitted rather impatiently. 'Can't I phone her back?'

Mrs Donleven made a little helpless gesture. 'She seems very keen to talk now. I did try to put her off, but . . .'

'Nothing puts off Lucy Templeton,' Elaine said resignedly. 'Right, I'll come.'

'Why not make us all some coffee while you're up at the house?' Rob called after her.

Morgana was afraid that Mrs Donleven was going to stay and talk to Lyall all the time Elaine was away. She was far too discreet, of course, to actually leap in the air for joy at the sight of him, but she did shake hands, according him one of her least chilly smiles. Morgana decided she was being unfair. Mrs Donleven wouldn't have been human not to welcome the arrival of anyone as attractive and eligible—and interested—in her daughter's life.

But there was no problem. Bartram's Babe began to toss his head and sidestep, and Mrs Donleven was nervous of horses, even in their predictable moments, and made haste to excuse herself and return to the house.

Rob turned to Morgana. 'Well, love, do you want to risk your neck on Babe for five minutes?'

'Try and stop me!' she smiled back at him. 'That's if Lyall won't find it too boring.' Her eyes, innocent, questioning, moved to Lyall's face. 'Unless, of course, you'd like to ride Babe yourself.'

'I won't deprive you of that pleasure,' he said, lifting an indolent shoulder.

As if the thought had just come to her, she said, 'Why don't you come and ride with me?'

'No, thanks. It isn't my favourite form of exercise,' he returned casually.

She saw Rob look slightly relieved and said hurriedly, 'Oh, you can't come to a stables and not ride. Rob will find you a quiet, safe mount if you're worried of making a fool of yourself in front of Elaine. Although you shouldn't be, because she's quite used to novice riders, you know.'

His eyes raked her, glinting. 'I wouldn't describe myself as a novice, precisely.' He looked at Rob. 'Which one do you suggest?'

Rob hesitated, clearly unhappy. 'Well—I suppose——' His eyes met Morgana's and he said reluctantly, 'Why not try Checkmate? You were admiring him earlier.' He gestured towards the box.

'Fine,' Lyall said with a shrug. 'If you'd like to show me where his tack is kept.'

'Oh, I'll do that,' Rob broke in quickly. 'We—we teach pupils to saddle up, but we don't expect our guests to do so.'

Lyall looked faintly surprised, but he only said, 'As you wish.'

Morgana's hands were shaking so much she could hardly slide the bit into Bartram's Babe's mouth. He seemed to sense her turmoil and moved restively, shaking his head, and she murmured, 'Easy, boy, easy,' and leaned her forehead against his neck for a moment.

She watched Rob lead Checkmate out into the yard. He came picking his way gracefully, the picture of amiable docility. When Rob had first acquired him, and his true nature had started to reveal itself, Morgana had joked they should re-name him 'Snake in the Grass'.

Now she ran her tongue over lips suddenly dry with apprehension, wishing that she'd never started this. In a way, it would have been a relief if Elaine had returned and given the game away.

'You go into the paddock with Babe,' Rob called to her. 'Give him a few circuits, then try him over a couple of jumps.'

She nodded and mounted, but her pleasure in the morning had gone. She had begun something, but she could no longer control how it might end. She wanted to see Lyall brought low, wanted to see him dishevelled with grass and mud on his immaculately expensive denim pants and black cashmere sweater, but that wasn't all she wanted. The fact was that he was attracted to Elaine, an expert rider, and would want to shine in her eyes, so his overthrow would be doubly humiliating was a bonus point.

She was hurting so much inside that she wanted him to be hurt in turn, and she knew that being held up to ridicule, being made to look a fool, would make him vulnerable. He was a successful man, a powerful man in all sorts of different ways. She wanted, just for a moment, to shake that implacable shield of power and competence that surrounded him, but at the same time she was frightened.

She recalled her disturbed thoughts. Riding an unfamiliar horse demanded one's whole attention, not just part of it, and Babe was already beginning to sidle and take liberties. She brought him firmly under control before they turned into the broad grass paddock, and he responded well to the mastery of hands and knees, walking, trotting, then breaking into a canter at her unspoken command.

She was almost starting to enjoy herself when she saw the others coming. She drew rein, and waited, her heart thumping. Checkmate seemed to be behaving impeccably, but any moment that could change, and Rob, who was riding a placid grey called Bunter, gave her a grim look as they entered the paddock.

'You realise Elaine will kill me for this,' he muttered out of the side of his mouth as he drew level with her. Morgana wanted to say something flippant or reassuring or both, but at that moment Checkmate erupted into life. Whinnying violently, he reared up, then bucked, kicking out with his back legs in an effort to dislodge his startled rider.

Morgana put a hand up to her mouth, watching in a kind of fascinated horror as Checkmate went through his malevolent repertoire. Lyall was hanging on grimly somehow, but any moment now he would be thrown. He had to be.

She closed her eyes. suddenly aware that she didn't want to see the *coup de grâce* when it came. Somewhere in the background she heard Elaine's voice, shrill with apprehension and anger, demanding, 'What the hell's going on here?'

Rob said hoarsely, 'Whatever he may have said to you, he wasn't bragging. My God, he can ride—he's fantastic!'

Dazed, Morgana opened her eyes, in time to see Lyall heading Checkmate, still breathing out outrage and venom, towards the low paddock fence, and the moor beyond. The chestnut cleared it effortlessly, then galloped on.

Morgana exclaimed, 'He's bolting!'

'Of course he isn't,' Rob said roundly. 'He's met his match at last, that's all.'. He threw back his head and laughed. 'Who'd have thought it?' He gave Morgana a faintly malicious look. 'I'm afraid your little scheme has come unstuck, my sweet.'

Elaine arrived looking as if she could eat broken glass. 'Whose bloody stupid idea was that?' she demanded. Her eyes blazed at Morgana. 'Or need I ask?'

'It was a joke,' Rob interposed hastily, gentling Bunter, whose stolidity was taking exception to the raised voices and uproar he sensed around him. 'And no harm done.'

'But no thanks to either of you!' Elaine's face was pale with rage. She wasn't dissembling. There was real bitter dislike in her eyes as she looked at Morgana. She turned on Rob. 'Well, aren't you going after him?'

'There's no need,' Rob said decisively. 'You could see that for yourself.' He laughed again. 'Check to old Checkmate! Well, well. Perhaps he'll make us an offer for the bloody animal.'

It wasn't a line of argument to pacify Elaine, who was

drawing breath for a new onslaught. Morgana said hastily, 'I'll take Babe back to his box.'

'That's an excellent idea,' Elaine snapped. 'And I have an even better one. Just keep away from my horses from now on, and from these stables, you vindictive, irresponsible little bitch!'

Morgana felt all the colour drain from her face. And the worst of it was she couldn't in fairness deny the epithets which Elaine had flung at her. They were fully justified.

Rob, very red in the face, said, 'Oh, calm down, for God's sake. It was as much my fault as Morgana's. I could have refused to let Lyall ride the horse—or warned him. Not that my warning would probably have made a great deal of difference,' he added. 'I imagine he would have seen it as an additional challenge.'

Morgana laid a hand on his arm as she prepared to ride Babe back to the yard. 'It's all right,' she said in a low voice. 'Elaine has every right to be angry. I've behaved like an idiot and made nothing but trouble all round.'

She didn't wait to hear any more, but urged Babe forward. Her one thought was to get back to the yard, complete the ritual of unsaddling and caring for the horse and be gone back to Polzion before Lyall got back.

Even if he hadn't already guessed her part in his unexpectedly rough ride, she knew that Elaine could hardly wait to tell him, and she couldn't blame her. But on the other hand, she didn't really want to stick around to bear the brunt of Lyall's immediate reaction, she thought.

Moving rapidly, she unsaddled Bartram's Babe, rubbed him down, and covered him with a light blanket. She checked that there was water in his bucket, gave him a valedictory slap on the rump as she left his stall, and walked towards the yard door.

Tall and narrow, the shadow lay across her path, and although even before she looked up she knew whom she would see, she could not stifle the involuntary cry that rose to her lips as Lyall left the doorway where he had been lounging and walked purposefully towards her.

CHAPTER SEVEN

MORGANA took a step backwards. It was an instinctive reaction, no matter how much she might tell herself that she was being foolish, or that Rob or even Elaine were probably within call, or that the most she had to face was another telling off.

She said, forcing her voice to flippancy, 'Enjoy the ride?'

'It was enlivening,' he drawled, and there was a note in his voice which made her pulses beat heavily and unpleasantly. 'I suppose I should have realised. Checkmate. Death to the King. Or didn't you intend things to go quite that far?'

She shrugged. 'Of course not—and they didn't.'

'But no thanks to you,' he said, too gently. 'You thought I was a comparative beginner, that I barely knew one end of a horse from the other.'

'You let me think so.'

'No,' he said. 'This time it was your turn to make assumptions, and wrong ones at that.'

'So it seems,' she shrugged. 'Can I consider my wrist has been slapped, and go now, please?'

'Like hell you can,' he said. 'And for the record, it isn't your wrist that I'll be slapping.'

'Don't you dare lay a finger on me!' Morgana said huskily.

'Not a finger, lady.' Lyall took a step nearer, and she was forced to retreat again. 'My whole hand, and hard. Call it retribution for the bruises you'd planned for me.'

He wasn't just threatening, she realised with a kind of sick dread. He really meant it. She tried to scream 'Rob!' but the only sound that emerged from her closing throat was a kind of strangled croak.

'He won't hear you.' There was scorn in Lyall's voice. 'He's still down at the paddock. I left the horse down there with Elaine and walked up. I felt you'd prefer your medicine in private.'

There was the faintest chance that if she moved fast enough she might be able to dash past him and to the door. What she would do after that, she didn't even stop to think. But even as she tensed, her eyes going to the open doorway and the beckoning sunlight, Lyall shook his head.

'Don't even try it,' he said succinctly.

Morgana couldn't retreat any more. The upright which supported the partition between two of the stalls was digging into her back, and the horses were getting restive. They might kick out.

As she hesitated, he reached for her, dragging her off balance. She gave a cry of alarm, snatching at his sweater in an attempt to steady herself, but he was moving too, going down on one knee and pinioning her across his bent leg, both wrists captured behind her in a grip of iron.

It was the worst humiliation of her life. His hand rose and fell half a dozen times, stinging her flesh even through the tough denim, as she writhed and jerked unavailingly, trying to evade him.

When he released her there were tears on her face, but more from shame and anger than actual pain.

'You swine!' she raged as he set her on her feet.

'I can think of some harsh words for you too.' He didn't show the slightest sign of repentance as she rubbed her wet eyes childishly with her fists.

'I wish he'd thrown you,' she cried. 'I wish he'd broken your damned neck!'

'Yes, I'm sure you do,' he shrugged, his eyes narrowing. 'I'm sorry to disappoint you, Morgan le Fay, but I've no intention of dying just so that you can get your hands on that mouldering pile of stones you call Polzion. Because you wouldn't have it for long, and you know that as well as I do. Your creditors would start pressing, and you'd be sold up, lock, stock and barrel. You'd lose it completely. Or is that what you want?'

'I've lost it now. I've lost everything.' All her passion, all her bewilderment at the turn of events was in her voice. 'You've taken it all. Oh God, I hate you!'

'As you've already made clear.' Lyall's voice was grim. 'Well, that's something you're going to have to live with, Morgana, because I'm here. I'm a fact of your existence, and I haven't finished taking yet—not by a mile.'

He stepped forward, and her hands flew up to ward him off. But it was too late.

In its way, his kiss was as merciless a punishment as the beating she had suffered at his hands. She moaned feebly under the insistent harshness of his mouth, as he forced her lips apart. His hand in the small of her back ground her body against his, giving her intimate and indisputable proof of his physical arousal. His other hand was lifting the edge of her sweater, and sliding beneath it, his fingers spreading across her rib-cage and upwards to find the tiny clip that fastened her bra in the cleft between her breasts and release it.

Morgana gasped helplessly. She couldn't breathe. She could barely think. And somewhere deep inside her a small hot flicker of wild, degrading excitement was beginning to build to a flame.

Lyall's hand cupped her bared breast, his fingers stroking the rosy peak until she thought she would faint with pleasure. The arm that held her pinned against him was no longer a prison but a delight. She wanted to be closer yet. For the first time in her life she wanted to be naked in a man's arms, for every inch of her to be bared and offered for his caresses. She wanted the secret knowledge of his own flesh under her hands.

And all the time the bruising kiss went on, drinking her dry, draining her will to resist. In the stalls behind her the horses moved, stamping their feet, and whickering softly. Above their heads a small bird flew crazily around the rafters, uttering cries of alarm. And in the distance there were voices.

Lyall heard them. He lifted himself away from her with a faint groan, pushing a hand through his dishevelled hair. His eyes were fever-bright as he looked at her, but his voice was cool as he said, 'They're coming. You'd better tidy yourself.'

The blood rushed into her face. She didn't want to

have to see anyone. She could imagine only too well the
sort of appearance she presented, mouth swollen, eyes blurred with unfamiliar passion, but she felt incapable of movement. Her body was weak, as if she had been battered in a
strong sea, swimming against a current which was too fierce,
too masterful. She was still gasping for breath, and even
the rhythm of her body, the sure beat of her pulses seemed
to have altered in some strange and fundamental way.

She said in a voice she barely recognised, 'I—must go
home.'

'I'll drive you.'

'No!' Her voice rose and cracked. 'No, I'll walk.'

She needed to walk. She needed to move, to make her
sawdust limbs obey her, to breathe deep lungfuls of moorland air, to regain in some small measure her equilibrium.

And, more important, she didn't want to be alone with
Lyall, especially in the confined passenger space of a car.
His touch could break her, she knew that now. His kisses
could turn her blood to fire. There must be no more of
them.

She looked down at the cobbled floor, and felt sick with
self-disgust. He would have known, of course. He was far
too experienced not to realise the effect that he'd had on
her. And the fact that he had been similarly aroused made
no difference at all to her sense of shame. After all, he had
never made a secret of the fact that he wanted her. It was
she who had flung her denial, her rejection in his face.
And now he knew she was his for the taking.

Lyall said abruptly, 'If you don't want to face them, I'll
head them off. Will you be all right?'

'Wonderful.' Morgana invested the word with all the
bitter irony of which she was capable.

He said, 'I didn't intend this.'

'Which? The—assault, or the interruption?' Her voice
shook. 'On second thoughts, I'd rather not know. Now,
may I go, please?' She still wasn't looking at him. She
never lifted her eyes, so she could only sense that he had
turned and gone, and that she was alone.

The next few days were some of the most difficult in her life.

She had thought she had reached her lowest ebb after her father's death when they learned what was to happen to Polzion, but she had been wrong. And the worst of it was that she had no one with whom to share her unhappiness.

She had to play a part—to act that her feeling towards Lyall were unchanged, that he still aroused cool dislike and distrust in her. And, she supposed, it was true that she did not trust him, but then she no longer trusted herself. That was the shattering blow he had dealt her—or rather,- the first of them, and the only one she could face.

It was hard having to carry out her duties in the hotel, when all she wanted was to hide in her room and never have to see anyone again. The only way she could survive was to turn herself into a kind of automaton, who worked and spoke, and even occasionally smiled as if she was pro- grammed by some inner computer.

She was thankful that her mother's preoccupation with the plans for Polzion prevented her from noticing that all was far from well with her daughter's emotional life. She would have been concerned, and might have asked ques- tions for which Morgana would have been unable to find answers—or at least answers the implications of which she would be able to bear.

She could not fool Elsa, of course. She had been an- swering her at random, one morning, too immersed in her painful inner world to pay much attention to the reality around her, when the older woman had snapped at her, and Morgana had burst into tears. It hadn't been that much of a shock. Elsa had been at Polzion for a great many years, and tended to spare no one the rough side of her tongue when roused, so she should have known what to expect. But she was unprepared for what happened next. Elsa gathered the shaking girl into her arms and began to soothe and pet her as if she were a small child again.

'There, my lovely, there, my handsome, don't take on so. 'Tes pain and woe, like I told you, and change and turmoil, but there it is, and it won't last for ever.'

No, Morgana thought, nothing lasted for ever. Not agony, not hatred, not even love. Even the mention of the word was enough to make her flinch.

She did her best to keep out of Lyall's way, but every glimpse of him, even the sound of his voice in an adjoining room was enough to send her pulse pounding.

It wasn't love, she assured herself desperately and with monotonous regularity. It was physical attraction, and totally transient. He had turned her world upside down in every possible way, so there was every reason for her to be aware of him.

She hadn't been sure what his reaction would be when he saw her again, and it had taken every scrap of courage she possessed to walk into the dining room that evening, and serve him his meal as if nothing had happened. And yet it seemed he was content with that. His manner was casual, verging on the aloof. There was nothing to indicate that this was the man whose passion had carried her to the brink of surrender only a few hours before.

But if that was the way he wanted it, then it was fine with her, she told herself defensively. In fact, it was ideal, considering that they had to work together.

Lyall had told her to her face that he hadn't intended that little scene in the stables, and she believed him. If he was honest, he was probably bitterly regretting it, especi-ally when they could so easily have been discovered by Elaine. She might not have been prepared to believe that he was making love to another girl simply because she had made him very angry. But there was no other explanation, and Morgana ruefully had to acknowledge that she had probably asked for it. She had behaved badly, and her punishment had turned into something uncontrollable.

As the days passed, she was forced to the realisation that Lyall was spending a lot of his time at Home Farm. He never said where he was going, or at least he never told her, although her mother seemed *au fait* with his movements.

It was Rob who confirmed her suspicions of where Lyall passed his days.

'It's quite amusing,' he said over a drink at the Polzion Arms one evening, although he didn't sound particularly amused. 'Mother and Father were considering making an offer for Polzion, and now it looks as if your cousin is about to take us over instead.'

Morgana sipped her shandy. 'What makes you think so?'

'Well, he's never away from the place,' he said rather irritably. 'That pleases Elaine, of course, but I can't say I'm particularly thrilled. He wants to know a little too much about the running of the stables for my liking.'

Morgana shrugged. 'Well, it isn't as if you've got anything to hide.'

'No,' Rob admitted. 'But let's just say that smooth operators like your cousin aren't my favourite sort of people.'

'I wish you'd stop calling him my cousin!' snapped Morgana with sudden fierceness. 'The relationship between us is so remote it barely exists. My God, he doesn't even use the family name, except when it suits him,'

'I think he uses everyone, and everything when it suits him,' Rob said dourly.

He was a better judge of character than she had ever given him credit for, Morgana thought drily. Because that was what Lyall had been doing, of course. It must have annoyed him to have encountered her dislike, so he had decided to amuse himself at her expense, until it bored him. Or until he met Elaine and realised that she would make a more entertaining companion, she thought, with an inward grimace of pain. Elaine spoke his language. She was used to his world, or at least the fringe of it. Even if he used and left her, she would survive. She was a great survivor.

Whereas I, Morgana thought, could well bleed to death for the rest of my life.

Rob asked with a touch of irritation, 'What's the matter, love? You spend most of your time in a trance these days. I don't seem to be getting through to you.'

'I'm sorry,' she apologised, flushing. 'What were you saying?'

He looked faintly mollified. 'I was asking if you were going to come to this party of Lucy Templeton's with me. It's a Hallowe'en do, and she wants us all to dress up.

It should be quite amusing.'

'Oh, I don't think it's my sort of thing,' she said quickly. 'Besides, Elaine will be going, won't she? I hardly think she'd be very pleased to see me there after what happened the other day—after the things she said to me.'

'Oh, come off it, love.' Rob looked a little uncomfortable. 'You mustn't take that much notice of what Elaine says. Her bark is always worse than her bite, as the saying is, and I'm sure she's forgotten all about that by now.'

'Do you?' Morgana was sceptical.

'Why, yes. In fact, she asked me if I was going to bring you to the party. That day at the paddock—she spoke in the heat of the moment. You should have heard what she said to me when she got me alone later!' He gave a rueful sigh.

Morgana put a hand on his arm. 'I'm sorry if I got you into trouble. It was a mad thing to do, and I should never have started it.'

'Well, it all turned out all right in the end.' He paused. 'Lyall really could be a first-class rider, you know, if he had more time to give to it. And he knows a hell of a lot about horses—more than I do, to tell the truth. If anything goes wrong these days, Elaine asks him his advice first.' There was a slightly sullen note in his voice, Morgana was quick to notice.

She said gently, 'I'm sure that Elaine does value your advice, Rob. It's just that Lyall is—a novelty.'

'I think she plans to make him a permanent fixture,' Rob said grimly. 'I don't know whether I could stomach him as a brother-in-law. But of course he may have his own ideas about that too.'

'More than likely,' she managed, past the sudden dryness of her throat. 'I—I didn't realise it was getting that serious.'

Rob shrugged. 'It all depends how serious is serious. I would reckon he's a man who likes to have a woman interested in him most of the time. Certainly he's not one of nature's celibates. But Elaine knows what she's doing, or I've always reckoned so. But I'm wondering whether she mightn't have bitten off more than she could chew.'

'What about your parents? What do they think?' Morgana ventured.

'Oh, they've gone back to London, but as far as my mother's concerned he has "eligible bachelor" written all over him, which I suppose he is on the face of it.' He sighed again. 'I wish he'd go away. Isn't he afraid that van Guisen-Lyall may collapse in a heap without him?'

'I don't think so,' Morgana gave a rather tight little smile. 'He spends at least an hour on the telephone each morning in the office, and there's a stack of mail for him every day. I think he manages to keep in touch. But I wish he'd go too. In fact I wish he'd never come here.'

It wasn't the truth. It would never be the truth again, but she justified her remark by wishing that it could be. The fact was that before Lyall came she had only been half alive. And when he went away again there would be a bitter, aching gap in her consciousness.

'Well, he'll certainly be here for the party,' Rob was saying. 'He's taking Elaine. Are you sure you wouldn't like to go?'

Recklessly she said, 'Yes—why not? It might even be fun at that.'

'And you could do with some jollification.' Rob peered at her. 'You've been looking a little peaky just lately, my love. It's understandable, of course, but I've been worried about you. You need taking out of yourself.'

He was trying to be kind, she knew, so she smiled at him, and let him hold her hand, and later he would want to kiss her and she would yield because she didn't want to hurt him, not that she had any desire to have his mouth on hers. His touch meant less than nothing to her now, so with each and every kiss she had to dissemble, because he was now showing every sign of wanting to carry things further each time they saw each other.

She knew she wasn't being fair to him. It would be kinder to tell him gently that she couldn't see him again. She could make some excuse about the pressure of work at the hotel which he could believe or not as he chose.

Yet she was reluctant to do it. Rob was her shield, the defence behind which she could hide her feelings for Lyall.

Being half of a recognised couple afforded her some protection. Once that was gone, she would be totally vulnerable, and Lyall would look at her and know the truth.

He might be amused—after all, it was quite amusing
that his casual ploy had had such devastating results. But
it wasn't what he had intended, she was sure. If she'd
been a different sort of a girl, she might have responded to
his advances and enjoyed the relationship which followed,
within its limitations. But she knew now that she wanted
Lyall without limits of any kind, and that anyway she
wasn't the type for a 'here today, gone tomorrow' lover.
It would be torment to have him, and then lose him, just
as it was torment to imagine him with Elaine.

But it was a torment she had to hide at all costs. His
amusement would be hurtful enough, but his pity would
be a thousand times worse.

Seeing him at the party, escorting Elaine, would be like
biting on an already aching tooth, she thought unhappily,
but it would be no worse than sitting at home alone, giving
full rein to her imaginings.

And Rob's admiration, his desire for her company, was
a salve to her bruised emotions. She wouldn't have been
human not to feel that. So she would go to the party with
him, and wear the brightest smile there, and no one would
be allowed to guess that her heart was breaking.

She was mad, of course, and she knew it, to be yearning
after a man who was still a stranger to her, and who
would probably have remained a stranger even after the
ultimate intimacy. She didn't fool herself about that.
There had been no real warmth, no gradual knowledge,
no touching of the spirit in what he had been offering.

But it would have been better than nothing, she thought
bitterly. Anything would have been better than that.

The surveyor arrived the following day, a tall, rather
serious man, much younger than Morgana had expected,
with gold-rimmed spectacles and a sudden engaging grin.
She had thought she would resent his presence in the
house, resent all the necessary poking and prying and
looking at plaster and floorboards and roof timbers, but it
was impossible to resent Paul Crosbie. He had a quiet,

laconic charm that was almost irresistible, and although he was thorough and looked at everything he wanted to see, at the same time he managed to be unobtrusive about it.

He delighted Mrs Pentreath by praising the house lavishly, admiring the cornices and the mouldings, and the decoration on the skirting boards which had no place in modern homes. It was clear that if he had his way, the character of Polzion would be preserved, and there would be no unsightly injections of plastic and chrome, or canned music, as Morgana had secretly feared. It was good to know that Lyall was a man of his word—that he wasn't going to cynically exploit the family home, because of past injuries.

He himself wasn't there. He had stayed just until Paul Crosbie had arrived and they had had a private conference in the office, and then he had gone off to Sweden, and Morgana had no idea when they would see him again, although she assumed he would be back at the end of the week for the party.

She found Paul pleasant company. He was writing a report on his findings and using the office, so she had to see quite a lot of him. Among other tasks, he was arranging to have Mark Pentreath's portrait cleaned, now that it had been brought down from the attic, and it was standing in a corner of the office carefully wrapped up, waiting to accompany him back to London.

'Family history's a fascinating thing,' he remarked cheerfully. 'I can trace mine back to the beginning of this century, but before that it's a big fat blank. It would be nice to go back and find that one was descended from— William the Conqueror, maybe.'

'It's sometimes a little disconcerting when you do know,' Morgana informed him candidly. She grimaced. 'We have our fair share of bad blood in the family. We could probably trace our origins back to Attila the Hun!'

He gave her an amused glance. 'That was said with feeling. I think I'd better not enquire too closely into what provoked it.'

She smiled. 'Afraid you might hear something derogatory about your boss?'

'About Lyall?' He sounded astonished. 'On the contrary. He's a great guy, both as a man and an employer. I couldn't ask for better.'

Her smile tightened. 'You should write his commercials.'

'He doesn't need them.' Paul put down his pen and studied her for a moment. 'I suppose it's natural that there should be a certain amount of friction between you. It can't have been easy, knowing that your home was going to someone you'd never met. But it could have been worse, you know. It could have gone to someone who would have sold it over your head, or just closed it up and left it to rot. And you wouldn't have wanted that to happen.'

'No,' she said dully, 'I wouldn't have wanted that.'

'Well then——' he paused. 'If it's any consolation, I've never known Lyall take such a personal interest in a relatively trivial project before. He's usually a great delegator. In fact I was surprised to find that he was still here. He's been cancelling a number of meetings, and postponing final decisions on all kinds of deals, and that's not like him.'

Morgana said, 'Perhaps he has other interests to occupy his attention.' Her voice was tart no matter how she might try to control it, and he grinned.

'You could be right. But she must be some lady if she's managed to take his mind off his work. No one's ever managed to do that before.'

'Have there been so many?' She tried to speak lightly, look amused.

'Enough.' Paul shrugged slightly. 'Hell, Lyall's an attractive man and he likes to play the field, and why not? Besides, I think what he saw in his own family life may not have given him an ideal view of marriage.' He paused, flushing a little. 'But none of this can be a surprise to you. After all, you're a member of his family, so you must know what the score is.'

'Not really,' said Morgana. 'He—he doesn't say much about the American side of his life, although I think he once told my mother that his parents' marriage hadn't been a great success. His father was a Pentreath, of course, my great-uncle's only son.'

'I'm afraid that's true,' Paul agreed. 'I know they were separated for some time before his death, and there were problems long before that. Lyall and I were at school together, and I can remember him getting letters from home that made him go very quiet.'

'He was at school in England?' Morgana asked helplessly. 'I didn't know that either.'

'He did part of his university training over here too,' Paul told her. 'I'm surprised he hasn't mentioned it.'

Morgana looked down at the small stack of bills she was paying—thanks to the transfer Lyall had made to the hotel's account in the local bank, their credit was good again.

'We don't talk a great deal,' she returned neutrally.

But Elaine would know, she thought. Confidences were all part of a love affair.

There was silence between them for a while, then Paul glanced up from his notes.

'Lyall said to be sure you were given the chance to go through all your grandmother's things, and see what, if anything, you wanted to keep,' he said. 'Would it be too much hassle if I had the trunks and other things brought downstairs for you? I'd like to get those attics clear, so that the roof timbers can be treated, and some repairs done. One of my colleagues will be coming down to make some sketches of the rooms for your flat, probably next week.'

Morgana hesitated. It would be much easier to tell Paul to dispose of the trunks along with everything else in the attic, but something held her back. There was a mystique about her grandmother's possessions which had always fascinated her, she thought. But then her grandmother had always fascinated her too, although she had never met her. Again and again as a child she had been drawn to that portrait upstairs, and the slim dark young woman with the smile of an enchantress.

It was no wonder that Grandfather, fierce as he had been, had fallen so deeply in love with someone so lovely and remote and vaguely mysterious, she told herself.

She said, 'There are some lovely clothes, but all terribly dated, of course. Lyall thought perhaps a theatrical costumiers?' Her voice rose questioningly, and Paul nodded.

'You decide what you want to keep, and I'll make arrangements for the rest,' he said.

A large van duly arrived to remove all the junk, but the trunks which were brought downstairs and lined up in the corridor outside her room. As she lifted the lid of the first one, and sniffed the faint aroma of lavender which drifted up from the folded garments, she felt like a child again, but this time no fierce old man was alive to terrify her with his accusations of meddling.

On the other hand, she did not feel totally at ease as she lifted and unfolded and gently set aside. There were some magnificent beaded and fringed evening dresses which would be a gift for anyone planning a revival of *The Boy Friend* or some other production set in the Twenties, she thought, and they were all immaculate. Even the blouses and skirts showed no sign of moths or wear and tear. She began to wonder whether her grandmother had ever thrown anything away. In the bottom of the second trunk there were other things besides clothes, she was almost relieved to discover. There was a photograph album, which she decided to study later, faded dance programmes, and stacks of letters tied into neat bundles. There was also a small leather writing case, which, rather to her surprise, was locked. Nor was there any sign of the key, although she searched right down to the bottom of the trunk.

And underneath everything else was a soft bundle, wrapped in tissue paper which disintegrated into soft feather strands as she touched it. She unfolded it and sat back on her heels, staring down at what she held in utter disbelief. Of all things, it was, it had to be the costume her grandmother had worn as Morgan le Fay. She shook it out, gently, and held it up to get a better look. There was no doubt about it, she thought, as her bemused eyes took in the low embroidered neckline and the long pointed sleeves, lined in contrasting silk. The colour had faded and was yellowing slightly along the folds it had lain in for so many years, but all the same it was in fantastically good condition. It was beautiful too, the dark green of woodland glades, with the gold embroidery dappling it like sunlight. There was a golden girdle too, which hung on the hips and was knotted loosely below the waist so that the long fringed ends trailed almost to the hem of the gown. There was a filmy veil too, to wear over the hair, and a tiny green and gold juliet cap to hold it in place.

She thought, 'This is one thing that's not going to any jumble sale or theatrical company.'

Acting on a barely understood impulse, she stood up and took it into her bedroom, holding it in front of herself, and studying herself intently in the dressing table mirror.

Rob had reminded her more than once that they were supposed to attend the Templetons' Hallowe'en party in some kind of appropriate fancy dress, but she hadn't been able to muster a great deal of interest in the idea. Not until now, she thought, seeing how the green of the gown darkened her eyes to emerald. There was a mounting excitement deep inside her. There would be a plethora of witches at the party, she had no doubt, all with steeple hats and dark cloaks and blackened teeth. But this would be incredibly different.

Hastily she stripped off her jeans and sweater and eased the fragile silk carefully over her head. It was a close fit. She was slim, but her grandmother must have been a sylph, she decided ruefully, turning sideways to view herself critically. But she could always alter the position of a few salient hooks, although she could do little about the rounded curves of her breasts swelling above the deep square of the neck. She was sure such conscious provocation would have been unthinkable in her grandmother's day. Probably a discreet frill of lace had been added then.

But the real Morgan le Fay wouldn't have bothered with such concealment, she thought. According to the legends, she was lady who relied on more than just magic for her enchantments.

She untied the ribbon that confined her hair at the nape of her neck and shook it gently, allowing it to fall forward on to her shoulders. A stranger seemed to look back at her, cool and dangerous with the knowledge of her own feminine power. The dress clung to every curve, accentuating her hips, and outlining the smooth line of her thighs.

She thought, 'It's no wonder Grandfather couldn't resist her.'

She stared at herself until the mirrored image blurred and swam under the intensity of her gaze, then she said aloud and fiercely, 'Grandmother—Morgan le Fay— teach me your spell. Teach me how to bewitch the man I love and bind him to me for ever.'

CHAPTER EIGHT

THE days leading up to Hallowe'en were busy ones. Paul Crosbie left, and Steven Chisholm, the architect, took his place. Morgana and her mother found themselves staring at an endless series of drawings showing them what the new flat could or should be like, and found themselves having to answer questions on their preferences in bathroom fittings and kitchen units.

Yet Morgana found it hard to show a great deal of interest in the project.

'You make the decisions,' she urged her mother. 'After all, it's going to be your home.'

'Yours as well, darling,' Mrs Pentreath protested.

'Only temporarily. I've agreed to stay a year—no more,' Morgana said stubbornly. The agreement was now in writing. Contracts had arrived, and been duly inspected by Mr Trevick and then recommended for signature. Morgana had felt trapped while she was doing so, but the terms had been more than clear, and if her mother was to have security then she had little choice.

'You may not want to leave,' Mrs Pentreath said serenely.

'Oh, yes, I shall.' Morgana's voice was grim. 'I want to leave right now.'

But was it really true? she asked herself as she tossed and turned at night, trying to find the sleep which constantly eluded her. If Lyall were to set her free from her promise tomorrow, would she really want to go—to sacrifice any hope of seeing him again?'

Perhaps hope was the wrong word to use, she thought, because she had little or nothing to look forward to from Lyall. Their relationship had been fraught with trauma from their first encounter, and nothing was likely to happen that would improve matters, least of all if she were to surrender to his casual lovemaking, to forfeit her self-respect for a few hours of sensual pleasure.

Longing for him made her body burn as if she was consumed by a fever. She was terrified by the strange pagan restlessness which seemed to be flowing in her veins, making her feel at one with the wind which howled round the Wishing Stone on the high moor, or sent the stormy breakers crashing over the rocks at the foot of Polzion cliffs.

She had changed her mind about the costume for the party. She had hung the Morgan le Fay dress in her wardrobe, and tried to ignore its presence there, telling herself it would be far more sensible to make herself a black steeple hat, and search through the outbuildings for the old besom broom, kept for sweeping leaves from the lawns.

Her grandmother's gown was dangerous, she told herself. It made her desire impossible things, gave her the illusion that she had the power to bring them about. The romantic aura which still clung to it had too much influence, she thought wryly, but she was a fool if she thought for one minute that the spell her grandmother had cast would work for her.

One evening, she and her mother had looked through the photograph album she had found in the bottom of the trunk, smiling over the faded sepia prints with the careful captions written below in copperplate handwriting.

'I suppose we can add this to the family records,' Mrs Pentreath said when they reached the end of the album. 'Some of them are fascinating, but it's a pity there are so many gaps.'

'Yes,' said Morgana, frowning a little. 'Did you notice that nearly all the gaps are photographs where Mark Pentreath was in the group?'

'No, I didn't,' said Mrs Pentreath, 'but then it's hardly surprising. I expect that your grandfather had them removed after the big row.'

'And the portrait sent up to the attic,' said Morgana, and sighed. 'My grandfather was a very unforgiving man.'

'Yes, he was, but there's always been a ruthless streak in the Pentreath men which emerges every generation or so. I was always thankful that your father seemed to have escaped it.' She looked wistful for a moment. 'Although I suppose for the sake of the business, it might have been better if he hadn't.'

'Well, for our sakes, I'm glad of it,' Morgana told her, and gave her mother's slightly dropping shoulders a swift hug. 'By the way——' she hesitated, 'there was a leather case among Grandmother's things which I've kept as well as the photo album. But the trouble is it's locked and I haven't found any trace of a key. When you were sorting out the keys of the house for Lyall, did you come across any spare ones that didn't have a lock to belong to?'

'Only one, but that was absolutely enormous. It wouldn't have fitted a small case.' Mrs Pentreath pursed her lips. 'I can't imagine why such a thing should have been kept.'

'Unless it contains something precious,' Morgana said slowly. 'It's heavy enough.'

'I can't think what that could be,' her mother shrugged. 'It certainly isn't your grandmother's jewellery. Every piece of that was sold.'

'Oh dear!' Morgana spread her hands in mock dismay. 'Does that mean no secret cache of diamonds? And there was I thinking we'd be able to buy back Polzion and tell Lyall to go to hell.'

'An attractive thought,' her mother said drily. 'But what makes you think he would sell? It's his home, after all. He has Pentreath blood.'

'And so much family feeling that he couldn't even be bothered to retain the name,' Morgana said too fiercely.

'There's an explanation for that,' Mrs Pentreath twisted her wedding ring pensively. 'From the time he was a small boy. I think he was imbued with stories of the Pentreath feud, and how his father and grandfather had been wronged. Giles, certainly, had an obsession about the house, and the fact that they'd been pushed out into the cold to make their way as best they could. Not that he did badly, at all,' she added, wrinkling her forehead. 'Lyall's mother was a rich heiress, but not even the knowledge of that could pacify him, and eventually there was a separation. It's hardly to be wondered at that Lyall grew to prefer to use his stepfather's name, instead of Pentreath which he associated with quarrelling and bitterness.'

'I suppose not,' Morgana said reluctantly. Her own childhood had been a relatively happy one. It disturbed her to think of Lyall coming from a broken home, no matter how luxurious.

Before she went to bed that night, she took the leather case from her dressing table drawer and studied it. She supposed if she wanted to know what it contained, then she would have to break the lock, and it was certainly far too heavy to be empty. She slid it back in the drawer and closed it decisively. She had too much to do and to think about to spend her time worrying about old mysteries and feuds.

And she would get rid of that dress, too, she thought. Every time she opened her wardrobe, the green silk seemed to glow out at her from the other rather sparse contents.

She walked across the room and took it out of the cupboard, tossing it carelessly over the back of her chair, regretting the impulse which had made her separate it from the rest of the things in the trunk. It was a dress that spoke of dreams and fantasies, and not the kind of reality she had to come to terms with.

Hallowe'en itself dawned with clear skies and a slight frost. The fierce wind had dropped overnight, and a crisp day held the promise of winter.

Morgana had just finished serving lunch and was on her way back to the kitchen for her own meal when the telephone rang. She was surprised to hear Elaine's voice asking abruptly for Lyall.

'He isn't here,' she said, rather taken aback. Although Lyall hadn't been in touch with them, she had supposed he would have maintained contact with Elaine, especially as they had a date for the party that very evening.

'Then where is he?' Elaine demanded. 'He can't still be in Sweden. He was due back two days ago.'

'I really don't know anything about his plans,' Morgana returned wearily.

'Is that a fact?' Elaine's tone was frankly sceptical. 'You're not being exactly helpful for a van Guisen-Lyall employee, you know. I hope you're not nurturing secret hopes of your own in Lyall's direction, because I can tell you now, sweetie, they're doomed to disappointment.'

Morgana was stung, both by the vulgarity of Elaine's remark, and its uncanny accuracy. Before she could stop herself, she said sharply, 'Because of your own hopes, I presume?'

'If you like to put it like that,' Elaine returned smugly. 'Stay in your own league, my pet. Rob seems reasonably besotted with you. Capitalise on that.'

'Thanks for the good advice.' Morgana's voice shook a little, and the knuckles on the hand holding the receiver were white with the strain of trying not to slam it back on the rest.

'You're welcome,' Elaine said negligently. 'Ask Lyall to call me when he does arrive, will you?'

'I'll be sure and make a note of it,' Morgana said ironically. 'Is there anything else?'

'Not at the moment.' She could hear the smile in Elaine's voice. 'But if there is, I'll let you know.'

Morgana replaced her receiver with deliberate gentleness and sat staring at it, fighting feelings which threatened to overwhelm her. Even in this comparatively short time, Elaine seemed to be very sure of herself and Lyall. Time alone would show whether this certainty was justified, and she would have to sit it out, trying not to betray by any word, look or gesture just how deeply her own emotions were involved.

She went back slowly to the kitchen where Elsa was waiting with some impatience to put a plate of steak and kidney pie in front of her.

'Now you eat that every scrap,' she adjured, standing over Morgana with her hands on her hips. 'You'm eating like a bird these days, and don't think I haven't noticed.'

'I'm really not very hungry.' Morgana reluctantly picked up her fork.

'No, nor very happy either—but there's better things on the way, maid.' Elsa gave a portentous nod. 'I looked at your tea-leaves this morning, when breakfast was done, and I saw a wedding ring there, clear as clear.'

Morgana gave a faint smile. 'I'm sorry to disappoint you, Elsa, but I'm not contemplating marriage.'

'Nor will you, till you'm asked,' Elsa pointed out reasonably. 'But there's a young man hungering for you at this very moment, and he'll be popping the question before you'm much older, take my word for it. The leaves don't lie, my lover.'

'Sometimes I wish they did,' Morgana said with a little sigh. She forced down another mouthful of savoury meat and rich shortcrust pastry, and nearly choked on an errant crumb as she noticed what was draped across the ironing board nearby.

'That dress,' she exclaimed. 'What's it doing down here?'

Elsa shrugged. 'I'm just giving it a little press. You can't go a party in a dress all creases.'

'But I'm not wearing it,' Morgana protested.

'Why ever not?' Elsa demanded. 'It's a proper handsome dress, and you won't see another like it.'

'That's the point,' Morgana said ruefully. 'I think I'd prefer to be lost in the crowd.'

'No sense to that, far as I can see,' Elsa sniffed. 'You wear it, maid, and knock your young man's eye out, just like your grandma before you.' She lifted the gown carefully from the ironing board and held it up in front of her. ''Tes your colour and all,' she added wheedlingly. 'And you can't waste all the work I've put in on it.'

'Which, of course, is the crunch,' Morgana conceded drily. 'All right, Elsa, have it your way. I'll wear the blasted thing. Just don't hope for too much. Perhaps men were more easily pleased in my grandmother's day.'

'And perhaps they weren't,' Elsa returned contemptuously. 'That's something that don't alter.'

Perhaps not, Morgana thought, but circumstances did, and her grandmother's happy love story with its lack of complication in no way resembled her own.

The same thought came back to haunt her, when, dressed for the party, she stood in front of her mirror that evening. She had been sparing with cosmetics, concen-

trating on adding extra shadow and allure to her deeply
lashed eyes, and the coolly exotic results, she thought
critically, fully justified the effort she had made. It seemed
a pity to have to cover the dress with her old grey cape.
Black velvet lined with emerald green would have been
far more appropriate.

Rob was waiting for her in the hall, tapping his foot
impatiently, but he smiled when he saw her coming down
the stairs. His brows rose slightly as he spotted the hem of
the green silk.

'Looks intriguing,' he commented. He moved as if to
open the grey cape, but she forestalled him.

'No—I want to surprise you.'

'You do that all the time.' He ran a caressing finger
down the line of her cheek, and she was hard put to it
not to flinch away.

'Shall we go?' She smiled up at him, making an effort.

'Yes, of course.' He hesitated. 'Elaine's waiting in the
car. We're giving her a lift to the Templetons'.'

'Oh.' Morgana bit her lip. She didn't particularly want
to face Elaine, who had rung up twice more during the
afternoon in a plainly deteriorating temper. 'She—she
didn't hear from Lyall?'

'A message from a secretary to say he couldn't make it.'
He frowned. 'Pretty casual, I must say. Fortunately
Jimmy Templeton's home on leave at the moment, and
he's an old flame of hers, so she won't lack consolation.'

But Elaine displayed scant signs of being consoled. She
barely spoke to Morgana as she got into Rob's car, and
remained silent during the drive to the Templetons'
house.

It was a large Georgian building, set squarely at the
end of a long gravelled drive, and hidden from the road
by a plantation of young trees. Coloured lights had been
festooned from these, and grotesque turnip lanterns
illuminated the gravel sweep in front of the house.

Lucy Templeton, a tall, rather horsy girl with a loud
laugh, welcomed Rob and Elaine effusively, and Morgana
rather more coolly.

'Darling, how utterly lousy for you,' she bawled at

Elaine. 'Still, your loss is Jimmy's gain, I suppose. Rob, my sweet!' She flew at him, twining her arms round his neck and giving him a lavish kiss. 'How simply marvellous! Long time no see,' she added in a lower tone.

Morgana was made uncomfortably aware that before Rob had started dating herself he had been seeing quite a lot of Lucy Templeton. He'd always given the impression that there had been nothing serious between them, but now she couldn't help wondering whether this had also been Lucy's view. Somehow, as she watched the avid way the other girl's eyes fixed on his face, she doubted it. She wished it was possible to take one's hostess to one side and say, 'Look—you want him? You have him.' But to do so would be to offer an intolerable insult to both Rob and Lucy.

Elaine had already stalked on ahead to leave her coat in the bedroom which Lucy had designated as the cloakroom. When Morgana entered, she was seated at the vanity unit adding a last touch of gloss to her already perfect mouth. The look she sent Morgana in the mirror was enough to chill the blood.

She said, 'I suppose you're feeling very pleased with yourself.'

'Not particularly,' Morgana said wearily, unfastening her cape and putting it down on the bed with the others. 'I don't suppose you'll believe me, but I'm sorry Lyall let you down.'

Elaine gave a mirthless laugh. 'Your sympathy is about the last thing I want! And it's quite unnecessary, I assure you. If and when Lyall does turn up, he'll learn that I don't sit around waiting for any man.' She thrust her glosser back into her evening bag, and closed it with a sharp click, before getting up abruptly and leaving the room.

Morgana let her shoulders sag a little in a kind of relief. She and Elaine had never been friends, but now the atmosphere between them was positively abrasive. She opened her bag and took out the little cap which matched her dress, and the drift of chiffon veil, and arranged it on her hair. Elaine, she had noticed, had not been wearing any kind of fancy dress. Her raw silk evening gown belonged strictly to the present day, and relied less on Hallowe'en magic than on the more potent allure of a deeply slashed neckline, emphasising the fullness of her breasts.

Morgana sighed. She wished with all her heart that she had also worn an ordinary dress, instead of being tempted to enter the realms of fantasy. But it is a fancy dress party, she tried to bolster her waning confidence, and I won't be the only one making a fool of myself.

But when she emerged rather shyly from the bedroom to find Rob waiting for her, the dazed expression in his eyes told her more clearly than any words that she was far from making a fool of herself.

He said unsteadily, 'My God, you look fantastic!'

'Well, don't sound so surprised.' she said teasingly. 'At midnight I change back into my usual rags, so we'd better go and find this party before the witching hour strikes.'

No expense had been spared to ensure that the guests who thronged the ground floor should enjoy themselves, Morgana soon realised. One of the rooms had been turned into a disco, with the equipment providing the music set on a raised platform at one end, where a cauldron steamed over a mock fire. The walls had been draped in black, and what lighting there was had been diffused through green filters. In the nearby dining room, a magnificent buffet had been laid out, and from a bar in the corner of the drawing room Mr Templeton, Lucy's father, was dispensing drinks with a lavish hand as an alternative to the deliciously spiced mulled wine being provided in the main hall. Nor had the younger ones been forgotten. Bobbing for apples was going on, accompanied by a lot of splashing and squeals of delight in a corner of the hall.

As Morgana had suspected, nearly all the girls at the party had opted for witches' gear, while Rob, in an evening cloak, and appropriate smears of tomato ketchup, was one of a number of Draculas among the men.

Morgana's own costume caused something of a stir, and a number of people, including Mrs Templeton, admired it, and asked her where she had got it.

'You're the loveliest girl here tonight,' Rob murmured to her at one point as they stood watching the dancers.

She smiled slightly. 'Lovelier than your sister?' She indicated where Elaine shimmered in her exotic golden silk, her arms twined provocatively round the neck of a clearly besotted Jimmy Templeton.

'Oh, Elaine has her moments,' he admitted casually. 'But it's you that's knocking everyone's eyes out tonight. You must have noticed, or have you only eyes for me?' It was said jokingly, but Morgana could not miss the serious, rather wistful note in his voice, and wondered if Rob was aware just how many times her glance had strayed towards the front door each time it opened to admit a new guest.

'Only for you,' she said quickly, but keeping her voice light.

'That's good.' His own tone deepened, became husky. His arm closed possessively round her waist, and he drew her nearer, bending towards her so that his breath fanned her ear persuasively. 'You know how I feel about you, don't you, darling? I wasn't going to say anything—not so soon after your father's death, but I've got to tell you.'

'Oh, Rob!' Something very like panic tightened her throat. 'Not here—not now.'

'I don't want an answer now,' he insisted softly but vehemently. 'Just think over what I've said, darling, that's all I ask. I won't rush you. I'll wait until you can be sure—until you're ready. After all, you don't want to work for Lyall van Guisen. I know you don't. I've seen your face every time it's been mentioned.'

Morgana made a wry face. 'So you're offering me an acceptable alternative?'

'It's more than that, and you know it. I love you, Morgana, and I want to marry you.' He paused, and then said with a trace of irritation, 'For God's sake let's get away from this row and find somewhere we can talk privately.'

His hand gripped her arm, urging her to go with him, but she resisted.

'Don't be silly,' she protested with a little laugh. 'We're at a party. There's no privacy anywhere. I don't understand you tonight, Rob. You've never been like this before.'

'And neither have you,' he countered rather roughly. 'I've always found you attractive, Morgana. I've always wanted you. But tonight you're beautiful. You've hexed me—got right under my skin. Tell me that you feel the same—that you'll think about what I've said.'

'I'll think about it,' she promised painfully. 'But—Rob—I feel so confused these days. I can't guarantee that I'll ultimately want the same as you.'

'I don't want any guarantees,' he denied instantly. 'I love you, and I know I can make you love me in return.'

Morgana moved restively, aware that several curious glances were coming their way and also that Elaine and Jimmy were approaching, followed by a sulky-looking Lucy and a young man Morgana only knew by sight.

'Now then, you two!' Jimmy boomed cheerfully. 'You look far too solemn for a party. I must say you're looking exceptionally gorgeous tonight, Morgana, like some sexy mediaeval princess. I bet old Rob's having to fight the other guys off.'

He laughed, but Morgana noticed that Elaine did not share his amusement, even though she stretched her lips in a dutiful smile. Her eyes as they studied Morgana were sour and faintly surprised, like a jealous swan observing the unexpected transformation of an ugly duckling. Elaine, after all, was not used to hearing other girls openly admired when she was present.

'Not exactly,' Morgana returned, her own smile stilted. She liked Jimmy, but then most people did, because although not always tactful, he was invariably amiable.

'Where did you find the dress? Not in Polzion, surely,' Lucy asked.

'Not quite.' Reluctantly Morgana found herself recounting the dress's history, and its role in her grandparents' courtship.

'Quite a romantic story,' Lucy commented condescendingly when she had finished.

Elaine's voice cut across her harshly. 'I don't see anything very romantic about being so hard up for cash that you're forced to wear a second-hand dress to a party.'

In the shocked silence which followed, Morgana felt hot colour flood into her face. She saw Rob start forward, his pleasant face stiff with anger, and put a hand on his arm.

'Rob, it's all right,' she said softly and urgently. 'I—I think I'd like to go home now, please.'

Jimmy made an embarrassed protest, but she was adamant. Elaine's malice had soured the evening for her, as the other girl had fully intended it should.

She sat still and silent in the car while Rob fulminated beside her.

'Honestly, darling, I don't know what came over her. She isn't usually like this, believe me.' He sighed. 'I shall have a few words to say to her tomorrow!'

'No, please don't,' she begged. 'She dislikes me quite enough as it is. A lecture from you would only make things worse.'

Rob gave her a swift glance, his brows drawn together in a frown. 'But she doesn't dislike you,' he objected. 'She has no reason to.'

Morgana shrugged. 'Emotions aren't always rational. We—we just don't get along. Surely you must have noticed.'

He looked uncomfortable, and she guessed that he had indeed noticed, but, man-like, hoped the situation would go away if he didn't mention it.

After an awkward pause he said, 'You don't really know each other, of course. If you did . . .'

We'd be as sisters, Morgana silently supplied, with a wry twist of her lips.

She said gently, 'You mustn't hope for too much, Rob.'

'Oddly enough I don't want my only sister and the girl I love at each other's throats,' he retorted rather sullenly.

'No,' she said with deliberate lightness, resisting the impulse to retort that most of the hostility was on Elaine's side, and always had been. 'I can see it might create problems.'

'I'm being serious,' he said crossly.

'I know you are.' Morgana paused. 'Perhaps you want

to reconsider some of the things you said to me earlier in the evening.'

'That's the last thing I want.' His tone was vehement. 'I want you to marry me, darling, and soon. Elaine's attitude will alter altogether when she knows you're going to be her sister-in-law.'

'But I haven't said I will yet!' She was faintly alarmed. 'Rob, you said you'd give me time to think.'

'You can have all the time you need,' he said with a new confidence in his voice, and she realised he had no doubt about what her ultimate answer would be. She sank back into the seat, feeling utterly dismayed, unable to come to terms with this sudden change in his attitude towards her, the apparent intensifying of his feelings.

When they reached Polzion, he said hopefully, 'Coffee?'

Morgana said apologetically, 'Not tonight, Rob. I— I'm rather tired.'

'That's what you always say,' he complained moodily. He reached for her, pulling her into his arms. She allowed him to kiss her, but there was no response to him in her. She felt as if every warm, breathing sensation in her had been numbed, and she could sense his bewilderment and disappointment as he realised her.

She stood at the front door and watched until his car was out of sight, smiling and waving. She felt she owed him that. Then she relaxed with a deep sigh and let herself noiselessly into the house. She glanced towards the drawing room door, hoping against hope that her mother might still be up, as she often was, but the room was in darkness, apart from a few embers which still smouldered in the grate. She turned away from the doorway and went slowly upstairs to her room.

She put on the light, closing the door behind her, and leaning wearily against the panels for a moment. Then, as she glanced towards the dressing table, she gave an involuntary gasp. Two unlit candles in brass candlesticks had been placed there, flanking the mirror, and a large rosy apple on a plate reposed in the middle.

'Elsa,' Morgana thought grimly, not knowing whether to laugh or cry, and strongly tempted to do both. She'd hardly been more than a child when Elsa had first told her of the old Hallowe'en superstition whereby a girl who stood in candlelight, brushing her hair and eating an apple, would see the reflection of her future husband in the mirror. She didn't have to eat the apple, of course. She could put it under her pillow and dream of her lover instead. For several years she had carried out one ritual or the other with naïve eagerness, but the only face which had ever looked back at her was her own, and the apple under the pillow had given her a crick in the neck, so gradually she had let them lapse.

So why had Elsa nudged her to revive them this year of all years? 'She's probably been reading the cards and seen Rob's proposal, and is hoping to push me in the right direction,' Morgan told herself without amusement. She was sorely tempted to rid her dressing table of the whole caboodle with one sweep of her arm, but guessed the ensuing clatter would wake the whole house and convince everyone that there were burglars at the very least.

She pulled off her cap and veil and tossed it down on the chair, pushing her fingers through her hair. The unlit candles seemed to mock at her, accusing her of cowardice.

She thought, 'It's just a silly superstition, and I'm not going along with it. I'm too old to believe in such nonsense. I'm not a child any more. Elsa should be ashamed of herself.'

But even in her own ears, her words lacked conviction. And the apple looked delicious, she had to admit. There wouldn't be any harm in eating a little of it, she argued to herself. After all, her supper at the Templetons' had been interrupted, and she was still hungry.

A small inner voice which said that it would be far more sensible to go down to the kitchen and fetch a sandwich and a glass of milk she ignored. She picked up the box of matches which Elsa had left conveniently to hand and lit the candles.

There was something about candlelight, she thought dreamily, as she switched off the main light. It created its own pools of brilliance, and its own shadows too. She reached for her hairbrush and began to stroke it across her hair while with the other hand she picked up the apple and took her first bite. Its flavour was sharp but juicy, like all the other Hallowe'en apples she had ever tasted, and suddenly the years rolled back and she was a child, thrilled, hopeful and a little frightened too, peering into the shadows of the mirror, waiting for them to lift for one second of infinity and show her a glimpse of the future.

She bit into the apple again, and she was Eve—all woman, all tremulous longings, waiting for her lover to come to her. The hand drawing the brush through her hair grew languorous, and a slow tingle of pleasure ran from the nape of her neck to the base of her spine.

The candle flames flared upwards suddenly as if in a sudden draught, and she stood motionless, the apple falling from her nerveless fingers and rolling away across the carpet, as she looked into her mirror and saw, beyond reason and beyond doubt, Lyall's face.

CHAPTER NINE

MORGANA wanted to scream, but the sound choked in her throat, emerging as a kind of moan. At that moment, hands warm and hard and all too human descended on her shoulders, swinging her round.

'It's all right,' Lyall said roughly. 'I'm not a ghost that you've conjured up.'

'What are you doing here?' In spite of herself, her voice quivered.

He lifted an eyebrow. 'At the risk of sounding repetitious, this is my home—or one of them.'

'But no one knew where you were. We weren't expecting you.'

He gave her a sardonic look. 'You're not actually admitting that you might have missed me?'

'No, I'm not,' she said angrily. 'It makes no difference to me where you are or what you're doing, but other people have different views. Elaine Donleven, for instance.'

He shrugged. 'Where does she come into this?'

'Tonight is Hallowe'en,' she reminded him. 'You were supposed to be taking her to the Templetons' party.'

He smiled faintly. 'I wasn't aware I'd made any kind of promise about it—my plans were far too uncertain for that. I'm afraid the lovely Elaine tends to take far too much for granted—probably because she's so lovely.'

'Well, she was very upset,' said Morgana, wondering rather helplessly why she should be fighting Elaine's battles for her.

'Oh, really?' he said cynically. 'How very uncharacteristic of her. I'd have said she'd have immediately looked round for an alternative escort.' He paused. 'Well, am I wrong?'

'No,' she said reluctantly, aware that he was still holding her shoulders. She moved restively, and he released her.

'I'm sorry if I frightened you,' he said conversationally. 'I assumed you'd hear the door opening, but you were much too intent. What spell were you casting tonight?'

Morgana flushed, feeling a total idiot. 'No spell at all,' she denied.

'No?' He bent and retrieved the apple, handing it back to her. 'Finish your supper,' he suggested gently.

'I'm not hungry.' Suddenly she felt close to tears. 'And it's only Elsa's foolishness anyway.'

'It's more than just foolishness if it prompts you to stand around in the dark frightening yourself to death,' he said. 'If it's any consolation to you, you also startled me.'

'I don't see how,' she muttered.

'I was downstairs in the drawing room just now. I looked up, Morgan le Fay, and there you were standing in the doorway. For a moment I thought your grandmother's portrait had come to life. Where on earth did you find that dress?'

'It was in the bottom of one of the trunks, so I decided to wear it to the party. It seemed like a good idea at the time,' she said wearily.

'I'd say it was still a good idea.' Lyall looked her over slowly, and she felt her body grow warm under his all-encompassing gaze. 'Have you any idea what you look like?'

'Oh, yes.' Deliberately she tried to make her voice cool, and even slightly amused. 'A sexy mediaeval princess was one comment, but I feel just mediaeval at the moment, so if you're quite satisfied that I'm not a ghost perhaps you'd get out of my room, because I want to go to bed.'

He said quite gently, 'So do I,' and reached for her.

Morgana was too startled to struggle or even protest as he gathered her to him. His hands burned through the thin silk of the gown, and she could feel the texture of the suit he was wearing, the imprint of every button and fastening on his clothes on her skin as is she had been naked.

He kissed her hard and deep, bending her backwards so far that she thought her spinal column would snap. She tried to say 'No,' but his invasion of her mouth was too total, too ruthless. Speech was impossible, the simple act of breathing nearly so.

When his mouth left hers to travel the length of her slender throat, it was a reprieve, but only a shortlived one, she thought dizzily. The movements of his lips on her skin were devastating, plundering a response she could neither understand nor control. Her arms went up to twine round his neck, her fingers twisting almost convulsively in his hair, and she heard him give a groan of satisfaction.

At last he tore himself away from her. His eyes burned down into hers. He said thickly, 'My God, these last days have been endless! I couldn't get you out of my mind for a moment in Sweden. You even kept me awake at night.' He laughed unsteadily. 'You're the first lady who's ever done that by being absent.'

She said in a low voice, 'Lyall—let go of me, please.'

'Don't be a little fool. That isn't what you want, and you know it.' He kissed her again with a searching warmth that left her pliant and gasping in his embrace. 'And it isn't what I want either,' he murmured against her lips.

'Wanting isn't enough,' she pleaded, trying to think coherently against the drugging sensations that his kisses were evoking.

'I'll make it enough,' he promised huskily. He ran a caressing finger across her lips, then stroked the line of her jaw, and the supple column of her throat. He drew a sharp breath and let his fingertips brush across the swell of her breasts above the square neckline of her dress. Her body arched in immediate instinctive response, and she heard him laugh deep in his throat.

'You don't need this dress,' he said. 'You wear silk already—every inch of you, my cool, beautiful witch.' His hand slid over her shoulders and down her back, making a nonsense of the tiny hooks and eyes on the bodice which she and Elsa had laboured to fasten. The dress slipped away from her, and she gasped, seizing it and pulling it up to cover her.

'Let it go,' he ordered. 'Unless you want me to tear it off you.'

He wasn't teasing. There was a note in his voice that warned her that he was deadly serious, and with a little helpless gesture she obeyed his order, letting the softness of the green silk drift down round her ankles, lifting her hands to cover her bared breasts.

'Don't hide from me,' he said quietly. 'It's too late for that, Morgana, and we both know it. You cast your spell and now we're both caught.'

It was true, she thought almost faintly. He wasn't holding her. He wasn't even touching her, but the look in his eyes was a potent caress, making her shiver and burn at the same time. She found herself swaying towards him, and with a little groan he reached for her.

His lips were achingly sensuous as they parted hers, and she returned his kiss without reservation, the slow sweet spiral of desire uncoiling slowly in the pit of her stomach. His hands cupped her breasts as if they were flowers, and she gave a whisper of pleasure against his mouth.

He whispered, 'Help me,' and she realised he meant with his clothes. Her fingers shook as she unbuttoned his shirt, curling her hand against the firm muscularity of his chest. He lifted her in his arms, burying his face in the warm valley between her breasts, his mouth and tongue moving erotically against her flesh. Morgana clung to him trembling, every nerve ending in her body alive and pulsating with a need she had never guessed existed. But she knew now, and she knew too that before Lyall had finished with her, every facet of that need would have been explored and fulfilled. She pressed her body against his, winding her arms and legs around him, answering his sensual demand with her own.

'Hellfire, Morgana,' his voice was harsh, 'I'm trying to be patient—I know it's the first time for you. Do you want me to blow what's left of my self-control completely?'

'Yes,' she whispered, burying her face in the curve between his neck and shoulder, overwhelmed by the scent, the taste of his heated, sweat-dampened skin.

'Then don't say you weren't warned,' his voice deepened and became husky.

He lifted and carried her, and she felt the yielding softness of her bed beneath her back. It was darker here, out of the range of the flickering candlelight, and she propped herself up on an elbow, looking for him. He had moved away to discard the remainder of his clothing, and with them he seemed to toss away the last vestiges of the smooth, civilised veneer he presented to the world. She realised that the feeling of power he emanated did not come merely from his wealth, or the size of the business empire he controlled. Stripped, he was physically tough, lean and muscular, broad at the shoulder, tapering down to slim hips. She stared at him, filling her eyes with him, while her pulse beats quickened and her mouth grew dry.

As he came back to bed, she said quickly, 'The candles.'

'Leave them.' There was a breath of laughter in his voice. 'It's too late for shyness now, lady, and it's my turn to look at you.' He lay down beside her, taking her face gently in his hands. He said, 'Each night in Sweden I used to torture myself picturing you like this, with your hair spread across the pillow.' He lifted a few strands to his mouth, pulling at them gently with his teeth, then let his hands slide the length of her body, lingering, caressing, arousing, while his mouth nibbled teasing, provoking kisses over her face and throat. Morgana was on fire for him. This was what she had wanted, she thought dazedly, to feel his body next to hers like this, and the reality was better than any imagining. Tentatively at first, then with growing boldness, she allowed her hands to begin their own exploration.

'God!' The word was forced from him almost convulsively. 'I want you so much, I've got to have you. Darling, I—I'll try to be gentle . . .'

'It doesn't matter,' she gasped, her fingers gripping his shoulders as he moved across her, and her eyes closed in surrender. Somewhere she was dimly aware of an alien sound, but all her absorption was centred on Lyall, on the exquisite sensations his hands and mouth were rousing, and all the satisfaction her body was screaming for.

So that when he jack-knifed away from her in a sudden tense movement, the shock was all the greater. She stared up at him, her eyes widening endlessly, realising almost incredulously that she no longer had his undivided attention, and at the same moment she recognised what the alien sound was. It was the front door bell, and as she listened unbelievingly she heard the sound of the knocker being vigorously applied.

Lyall muttered savagely, 'What in the name of God . . .' He swung himself to the floor, reaching for his clothes. He threw Morgana a glance in which impatience was pre-eminent.

'I'd put something on if I were you,' he advised drily. 'The whole house will be awake soon it that racket goes on.'

Her face crimsoned as his words registered, and she sat up in silence, grabbing for her dressing gown.

He went on almost conversationally, 'I take it you weren't expecting any callers at this hour.'

'Of course not.' To her amazement, her voice sounded almost normal. 'It's after midnight.'

Lyall looked at her with irony. 'I'm fully aware of that. The witching hour. Don't you think you should answer that door before someone knocks it down?'

Thrusting her feet into heelless slippers, Morgana fled from the room. At the top of the stairs she paused, trying to steady her breathing and regain a modicum of control over her shaking limbs. Below her, Elsa, massive in a flowered housecoat, was already making her way grumbling to the door. As Morgana reached the foot of the stairs, she had unlocked the door and drawn back the massive top bolt and was demanding truculently of the unseen caller, 'Whatever is it?'

She was thrust aside and Elaine Donleven, strangely dishevelled, almost fell into the hall.

She said thickly, 'Phone—I must phone. Jimmy's hurt.'

Morgana went to her. 'What's happened. Where is he?'

Elaine gestured, her breathing shallow. 'Down—by the gate. The car went into the ditch. He took the corner too fast.' She drew a long shuddering breath. 'He hit his head. I—must phone.'

'I'll do that,' said Morgana. She glanced at Elsa. 'Will you take Miss Donleven in the drawing room and bring her some tea?'

But Elaine was paying attention to neither of them. Her eyes were riveted on Lyall, who was coming slowly down the stairs.

She cried out, 'Oh, Lyall—darling!' and flung herself into his arms. sobbing hysterically.

He said quite gently, 'It's all right, Elaine. We'll see to
everything. You go with Elsa and try to keep calm. I'll go
down and stay with Jimmy while Morgana gets an ambulance and phones his parents.' He freed himself from her
clinging hands and turned towards the front door.

Her telephoning completed, Morgana went along to
the kitchen to see if the tea was ready. Elsa was still muttering darkly to herself, but the tea was hot and strong,
and the tray daintily laid.

Morgana said wearily, 'What a dreadful thing. Daddy
always said there would be an accident on that corner
sooner or later. But what on earth were they doing on this
road anyway? The turning for the Home Farm was about
a mile back.'

Elsa snorted. 'Off to the clifftop for a spot of canoodling,
of course.'

Morgana had never felt less like laughing in her life, but
the application of the word 'canoodling' to the elegant and
sophisticated Elaine brought à reluctant grin to her face.

When she carried the tray into the drawing room, she
found Elaine lying on the sofa with her feet up and a
peevish expression on her lovely face.

Elaine said sharply, 'Where's Lyall? Isn't he back yet?'

'I imagine he intends to stay with Jimmy until the
ambulance gets here,' Morgana returned pacifically,
pouring the tea and handing her a cup.

'But I need him here with me,' Elaine protested. 'I've
had a terrible shock.' She sipped the tea and grimaced.
'Ugh, it's got sugar in it!'

'For the terrible shock,' Morgana said drily, adding
some judicious pieces of wood to the still smouldering
embers in the hearth and coaxing them into a small blaze.

'Jimmy should never have been driving, of course. He'd
had far too much to drink,' said Elaine after a pause. 'I
wanted to call a taxi, but he wouldn't let me.' She shot
Morgana a venomous look. 'If Rob had been around,
none of this would have happened.'

'Are you trying to say this is all my fault?' Morgana
asked helplessly.

'Well, there was certainly no need for you to flounce off

like that,' Elaine said coldly. 'You're far too thin-skinned, my dear.'

There was an obvious retort to that, but Morgana forbore to make it. And at that moment Lyall came in.

He said abruptly, 'Templeton's father has arrived. He's going to stay with him until the ambulance gets here—not that it's necessary. I think he'll have a black eye tomorrow, but that's all. The car was the chief sufferer.' He looked at Elaine. 'Perhaps you'd better stay the night. Morgana will get a room ready for you.'

'Yes, of course.' Morgana rose from the hearthrug, tightening the sash of her dressing gown as she did so, desperately conscious that she was naked beneath it, and aware of Elaine's increasingly speculative gaze.

Her prime objective when she got upstairs was to put some clothes on. The act of putting on jeans and sweater and brushing back her hair, securing it at the nape of her neck with an elastic band, helped in some odd way. Physically and mentally, she ached, but at least she presented a cool and reasonably competent appearance to the world.

There was nothing at Polzion House to compare with Elaine's luxurious bedroom at the Home Farm, but Morgana did her best, and when the room was prepared with freshly aired sheets, and the bedside lamp lit invitingly, it had a comfortable if rather faded charm. Gritting her teeth, Morgana arranged her favourite nightdress on the bed, and added a spare toothbrush, still in its cellophane wrapping.

As she turned to leave the room after a last glance round, it was to see Lyall standing in the doorway watching her.

She asked, 'Checking on the suitability of the accommodation?'

'Not exactly,' he said. 'You and I have some unfinished business.'

She shook her head. 'No, we haven't. This is my business—the hotel business. This is what I'm paid for—what my contract stipulates I should do. It doesn't mention I have to submit to being seduced by the owner.'

'Submission was hardly what I had in mind,' he said. 'But you must agree that we have to talk.'

'We have nothing to talk about.'

'Don't be a fool,' he said bitingly. 'You know better than that. You haven't that short a memory.'

'All right, then—let's say I don't need any further reminders that I nearly made a total fool of myself tonight.'

'Is that how you look at it?' His tone was odd.

'How else?' she said shortly. 'Now please leave me alone, or I'll scream and give this house the second sensation of the evening.'

'Very well,' he said quietly. 'But our talk is only deferred. There are things I have to say to you.'

Morgana shrugged. 'But that doesn't mean I necessarily have to listen.'

He drew a long breath. 'Vixen! Stop punishing me. I didn't organise that interruption. Next time I'll make sure . . .'

'Next time?' Temper exploded inside her and her voice rose. 'Next time? There'll be no next time, you swine! I'll never let you touch me again. I must have been mad tonight, but I'm sane again now.'

'Are you? You sound pretty hysterical to me.' His tone had hardened. 'What do you intend to do? Try and pretend that tonight never happened?'

'Something like that,' she said savagely. 'Now perhaps you'd like to get back to your guest. She must be wondering where you are.'

She went along to her own room and sat on the bed, staring sightlessly in front of her.

Pretend that tonight never happened, she thought. If only she could! Elaine's unexpected descent on Polzion had been a blessing in disguise. It had provided her with a timely reminder that she was far from being the only woman in Lyall's life, and that all he was interested in was a casual sexual encounter, and if she'd ever allowed herself foolishly and childishly to hope for anything different, then she knew better now.

She wanted to cry, but she wouldn't allow herself to do that. She still had things to do, duties to perform downstairs. There was the rekindled fire to guard, and the tea things to clear away. She got up resolutely and opened her door.

The corridor outside was dark, the sole illumination being the light coming from Elaine's room. Elaine herself was standing in the open doorway, looking up at Lyall. She was smiling and every line of her body outlined by the glimmering golden dress was an invitation.

As Morgana watched helplessly from the shelter of her doorway, Elaine reached out and took his hand, drawing him into her room, and closing the door behind them.

It was quite dark now. Morgana crushed her fist against her lips, stifling the little moan which rose from her throat. Every dream was over. The witching hour was past, and the spell was broken for ever.

She was late down to help with breakfast the next morning, but her mother waved away her halting apology.

'I'm surprised you made it at all, darling, after your disturbed night. I can't imagine how I slept through it all, especially as Miss Meakins informed me pointedly that she hadn't managed to get a wink of sleep because of all the comings and goings.' She gave Morgana an affectionately critical glance. 'You look very pale, dear. Do you think you ought to go back to bed?'

'I'm sure I shouldn't,' said Morgana with a little wintry smile. 'Er—where is our unexpected guest this morning.'

'Having breakfast in bed,' Elsa interjected disapprovingly. 'The very idea! And freshly squeezed orange juice, if you please. She can have it out of a tin, same as everyone else.'

Morgana did not enquire where Lyall was. She did not want to think about him, let alone mention his name. She had thought too much during the long night, as she had tossed restlessly trying vainly to blot out the mental image of him holding Elaine in his arms, their bodies entwined together.

Now she said hurriedly, 'If you think you can manage, I'd like to pop down to the Home Farm for a while.'

She didn't wait for a response, but walked out of the house, pushing her arms into the sleeves of her jacket as she went.

Rob was just coming out of the stables as she drove into the yard and he stopped, eyeing her with surprise as well as pleasure.

'You're the last person I expected to see this morning,' he commented, as she got out of the car. 'You obviously kept off the mulled wine last night, and I bet Jimmy wished he had too.'

Morgana forced a smile. 'I bet! He was very lucky. They both were.' She thrust her balled fists into the pockets of her coat and said jerkily, 'Rob, I've come to say—to ask if you really meant what you said last night?'

He stared at her. 'I meant every word.'

She swallowed. 'I see. Then I just want you to know—I'll marry you. But not yet.' she added in sudden panic, as he took a quick stride towards her, his face lighting up. 'It's too soon—after my father's death.'

'Yes, yes, of course.' He tried to make his voice suitably grave and sympathetic, but he was grinning from ear to ear. 'Oh, darling, I won't give you a moment's regret.'

His arms closed round her and she shut her eyes as she submitted to his embrace. She tried to respond, to convert her liking for him, her affection even, into a physical warmth, but at the same time, something inside her was asking whether this was to reassure him or herself because the truth was that she felt nothing.

She tried to tell herself that she was simply drained after the previous night. Things will improve, she told herself fiercely, as he reluctantly released her and she drew away, trying to smile.

'I—I must go. I have a million and one things to do at the house.'

Rob leaned forward and kissed the tip of her nose. 'Well, if Elaine runs you ragged, warn her that she'll have me to contend with. I'll pick you up tonight and we'll go out to celebrate. Right?'

'Right,' she agreed. She didn't feel like celebrating, she thought as she drove away. She felt more like weeping. But after last night, she doubted whether there were any more tears inside her to shed.

She hated herself for what she had just done. She was

using Rob, using him in cold blood as a protection against her feelings for Lyall, as a defence against the agony of jealousy and despair which threatened to overwhelm her whenever she thought of him.

And she needed a defence. Last night had proved that once and for all. Where Lyall was concerned she was weak, totally without resistance, and she couldn't afford to be weak any more. She had fallen in love with Lyall, deeply and desperately, but there was no future in it, and never had been.

Yet with Rob there could be a future. He was good and kind and safe, and she was fond of him. All she could hope was that out of that fondness something deeper and more permanent might develop, if it was allowed to. And in the meantime he would be her shield and protector against Lyall.

She could learn to care for Rob in the way he would want, she told herself defiantly. She was capable of passion. She'd just never given him a chance, that was all.

I want contentment, she thought, and security. I don't want to feel torn apart inside when he touches me. I don't want to ache for him. But I'll make a firm foundation for our relationship; I owe him that at least.

She put the car away and slipped into the house by the side door, hoping to avoid seeing anyone. Sooner or later she would have to break the news about her engagement, but not yet. First she had to accustom herself to what she had done.

She went up the stairs lightly, two at a time, heading for her room, and came face to face with Lyall, who was standing alone on the gallery, looking at the family portraits. There was something different about the display, she realised, and when she looked more closely, she realised that Mark Pentreath's portrait now hung there, and some of the other pictures had been rearranged to make room for it.

'I hope you approve.' He glanced at her, eyebrows raised.

'It really makes little difference whether I do or not,' she said. 'But it seems only fair to restore him to his rightful place. It's a pity he was ever ousted from it.'

'He'd agree with you there,' he said ruefully. 'He was a man with an obsession.'

Morgana went to walk away, but he detained her. 'Feel like talking this morning?' His eyes were fixed on her face, and she felt the familiar, painful lurch of her heart.

'It rather depends on the topic of conversation.' She tried to keep her tone impersonal.

'The topic is you and me,' he said.

'You speak as if we were a pair,' she said sharply.

He smiled. 'Are you trying to pretend that we aren't?'

He had no idea, of course, that she'd seen him with Elaine the previous night. She took a deep breath. 'I'm telling you that we aren't. Be the first to know, Lyall. I'm engaged to be married.'

'The hell you are!' His voice bit at her.

'It's true.' She faced him, chin up. 'Rob asked me to marry him at the party, and I agreed.'

'I don't recall any mention of that rather important point last night.' His voice had lengthened to a drawl, but Morgana was not deceived by his apparent calm. His eyes were incandescent with rage.

She shrugged. 'I didn't agree last night. We actually became engaged about half·an hour ago.'

'Dear God,' he said quietly. He looked at her and she flinched inwardly from the contempt in his face. 'You're a fast worker, I'll say that for you. Melting in my arms one moment, and getting engaged to that poor devil the next. What would you have done if I'd actually had you? Eloped?'

Morgana lifted her arm and slapped him as hard as she could across the face. She was terrified when she'd done it. She could see the marks of her hand on his cheek, and he was angry already. She would have no one to blame if he retaliated and hard.

Instead he smiled, his eyes holding hers remorselessly. 'I won't wish you luck, Morgan le Fay,' he said. 'I'll save my good wishes for Donleven. He'll need them—married to a ruthless little bitch like you.'

Then he turned on his heel and walked away, leaving her there, smarting as if he had slapped her after all.

CHAPTER TEN

'You're engaged to Rob?' Mrs Pentreath's eyes searched her daughter's face in amazement. 'Darling, isn't this rather sudden?'

'Is it?' Morgana smiled, but inwardly she was discomfited by this lukewarm reception of her news. 'I've been going out with him for quite some time.'

'I know that.' Elizabeth shook her head. 'But I never thought your feelings were quite so deeply involved.'

'You don't sound very pleased. I thought you liked Rob.'

'I do like him. No one could really help doing so, but that's hardly important. It's your attitude—your emotions that matter.' Mrs Pentreath hesitated. 'Has he told his parents yet?'

'I imagine he's telling them now.' Morgana gave her mother a challenging look. 'Why? Do you think they'll have any objections?'

'I wouldn't care to hazard a guess,' Mrs Pentreath returned rather drily. 'You've had more contact with them than I have. Do you imagine they'll greet you with open arms?'

Morgana was silent for a moment, then she said defensively, 'I'm marrying Rob, not his family.'

'I suppose so,' Elizabeth said without conviction. 'Darling, I know you've been unhappy lately—unsettled, but things will improve, I promise. Don't do anything hasty—anything you might live to regret.'

'I guarantee that I won't,' Morgana said gently.

Elsa's reaction to the news was even more negative.

'My dear soul,' she said flatly, sitting down at the kitchen table, 'you must be mazed, that's all I can say.'

'Elsa,' Morgana protested uncomfortably, 'you've always said you wanted to see me happy and settled, and you saw a fair man in the cards.'

'Well, t'wasn't him.' Elsa said grimly. 'You know better

than that, maid, so don't deny it.'

Morgana's lips quivered suddenly and she avoided Elsa's gaze.

'It has to be him,' she said in a low voice. 'There's no one else.'

She turned quickly and left the kitchen.

After the response in her own immediate circle, it was too much to hope that Rob's parents would greet the news with delight. As it was, they were polite but cool, and the tight-lipped, defensive expression on Rob's face told its own story. When they left Home Farm, he drove to Newquay for dinner where they ate an extravagant meal completed by the champagne he insisted on ordering. They laughed a good deal, and drank a number of silly toasts, but the evening was not a great success. There was too much being left unsaid, Morgana thought as they drove home, but surely good and lasting relationships had developed from equally unpromising beginnings.

And tonight she would not get away with a plea of tiredness, she knew. She had agreed to become Rob's wife, and he would require some surety of that promise. She rested submissively in his arms while he kissed her, wondering dazedly what strange chemistry it was that could turn her blood to rivers of flame under one man's lightest touch, while the most passionately intimate kisses from another could leave her cool to the point of indifference.

He murmured her name, his lips urgent against her throat, and let her go with the utmost reluctance.

'Forget what I said earlier.' His voice was hoarse. 'I want to marry you as soon as it can be arranged. I don't want to wait.'

She said gently, 'I can't decide anything in a hurry, Rob—you must see that. We'll talk about it tomorrow.'

'When I've cooled down, you mean?' His tone held a note of anger. 'I'm sorry, Morgana, don't I switch off quickly enough for you? I want to marry you, don't you understand that?'

'Of course I do, but I thought you saw my point of view too.' She tried to smile. 'Rob, I'm barely used to being engaged yet.'

'Then I'll have to give you time,' he said heavily. He leaned forward, brushing her mouth with his. 'All the time you want, darling.'

Morgana let herself quietly into the house, feeling blank with relief. It had not occurred to her that the engagement she had regarded in the light of a sanctuary could suddenly become a trap.

The drawing room door was slightly ajar, and she could hear the murmur of voices. Noiselessly she crossed the hall and peeped in. Her mother was sitting there talking quietly to Major Lawson. It was a cosy, companionable little scene and Morgana was loath to interrupt it, so she decided she would go straight upstairs without saying goodnight.

As she reached the foot of the stairs, she heard a creak above her and, looking up, she saw Lyall walking slowly down towards her. She swallowed, and her heart began that slow confused pounding as she fought for self-control. She hadn't expected to see him. He had taken Elaine home after lunch and she had understood he was not expected back until late.

He said coolly, 'Had an enjoyable evening?' His eyes ran over her, missing nothing. 'You look curiously untouched,' he added insolently. 'He can't be a very demanding lover.'

'Unlike you, he doesn't confuse love with lust,' she said between her teeth. 'Rob isn't an animal.'

'Then he should think twice before tying himself up with a little wildcat like you,' he said too pleasantly. 'I still have your teethmarks in my shoulder.'

'I don't believe you!' she exclaimed, flushing indignantly.

Lyall moved as if to unbutton his shirt. 'Shall I prove it to you?'

'No!' She glanced round in agitation, remembering just how many other people and potential eavesdroppers there were in the house. 'Oh, leave me alone!'

'I'm not touching you,' he said, but he might as well have been, she thought miserably, her teeth tearing at the soft inside of her lip. Oh God, how long would it be before the memories and sensations of the previous night ceased to torment her?

He asked, 'Have you fixed the date yet?'

'Not yet, but I imagine it will be sooner rather than later.' She clamped her chosen defence securely around her.

'Really?' He raised his eyebrows. 'I thought he was a believer in long engagements.'

'You have no reason to suppose that.'

'No? I'd have called a year a long engagement these days—even for someone with his vile lusts as firmly under control as you seem to think.'

'Why on earth should we wait a year?'

'A little matter of a contract,' he said smoothly, his eyes intent on her face.

Morgana was taken aback, but she concealed it. 'You can hardly hold me to that under the circumstances,' she protested. 'Everything's changed.'

'I'll hold you to it under any circumstances, and you'd better believe that, lady,' he said softly. His smile widened. He was enjoying his triumph, she thought furiously.

She shrugged. 'I don't expect Rob will mind a working wife,' she said. 'It's quite usual these days.'

'I wouldn't be too sure of that,' he said drily. 'Anyway, the question doesn't arise. You remain single during the run of your contract.'

'You can't make me,' she said angrily. 'You haven't the slightest right. As long as I do my job properly . . .'

'Ah, but I couldn't count on that.' His tone was derisive. 'You might get a bad case of honeymoon fever and become totally inefficient—for my purposes at least,' he added.

'You can't stop me getting married.' Her eyes fixed burningly on his face.

'Don't push me, Morgana,' he said. 'Unless you want me to show your milk-and-water fiancé my dishonourable scars and tell him exactly how I acquired them.'

'He wouldn't believe you.' She had begun to tremble.

'I think he would—eventually,' he said. 'Especially if I gave him a sneak preview of what you look like without your clothes. That little mole on your hip, for example. He might not be too pleased to know that I'd seen it first.'

'Swine!' she choked.

'I've been called worse names,' Lyall said coolly. 'I like to win, Morgana—I thought I'd made that clear. And remember this too—while you work for me, you don't marry Rob. I have other plans for you, just in case they'd escaped your mind.'

'You're vile,' she said shakily.

'And you're becoming repetitious,' he retorted. 'Goodnight, Morgan le Fay, sleep well.'

Morgana affixed the silver star to the top of the Christmas tree, then dismounted gingerly from the stepladder to take a critical look at her handiwork.

Normally, as Christmas approached, she threw herself heart and soul into the preparations for it, but this year she had to admit she had never felt less festive in her life.

The fact that for the past six weeks the house had been full of workmen hadn't helped matters, she thought as she put the stepladder away. The central heating had been installed, and a full rewiring programme completed, while at the same time work had gone forward on the conversion of the attics.

'The power of money,' Mrs Pentreath had remarked helplessly one day, surveying the organised chaos around her. 'When you think of the difficulty we used to have in getting even the *smallest* job done . . .'

Morgana did think of it, often, as she watched money being spent without stinting around her. She wanted to feel resentful, she wanted to hate Lyall for demonstrating so effectively the gulf between them, but she couldn't. The truth was that in spite of the dust, the inconvenience and the general upheaval, Polzion House was slowly acquiring a comfort it had never aspired to before in its long history.

And if she had been able to conjure up some kind of resentment, it would surely have been allayed by the sight of her mother happily poring over wallpaper books and fabric samples.

The new flat at the top of the house would be ready for them to move into by Christmas, they had been promised, and for Morgana this move couldn't come fast enough.

Once the flat was finished, at least she would have some privacy, an escape route to solitude.

Over the past weeks it seemed as if she had never been alone. It was not just the house being full of workmen either. Rob either telephoned or came around every day, in spite of her attempts to dissuade him. She supposed ruefully that if she'd really been in love with him, she would have welcomed his visits and calls, and expected them, but as things were, they were just an added irritation to all the others she had to bear.

Miss Meakins had finally taken her departure, declaring tearfully that she could not stand being moved from room to room in the path of the workmen any longer. Morgana wished she could have felt regretful, but not having to listen to Miss Meakins' daily catalogue of complaints could only be a relief.

She had half expected Major Lawson to take his departure too, but he showed no signs of objecting to the constant upheavals which were part of everyday life at Polzion House, and Morgana had a shrewd idea why he was staying put. She'd noticed that his quiet after-dinner chats with her mother were becoming more protracted, and that they had slipped quite naturally into being on Christian name terms. She had also noticed that whether her mother realised it or not, she was starting to depend more and more on the Major's advice, and quote it triumphantly when she wanted to prove a point. She was undoubtedly beginning to look much happier, and although Morgana told herself this was probably due to having the financial burdens of past years so completely removed from her shoulders, she was sure that there were more personal reasons for the new optimism in Mrs Pentreath's smile and the shine in her eyes. And she was also sure that Elizabeth wasn't even aware that they existed, and would be very shocked and distressed if anyone was even to hint that the days of her widowhood were numbered, although Morgana knew that any such suggestion would be premature in the extreme. Her mother, thanks to Major Lawson's undemanding company, was happier and more relaxed than Morgana could remember her being for years, and there could be no harm in their relationship even if it never progressed beyond the present pleasant companionableness.

As for her own relationships—Morgana bit her lip painfully—the last few weeks had been almost more than she could bear. Since their last confrontation when he had smilingly told her he intended to hold her to the letter of her contract, Lyall's attitude to her had undergone a radical change. His treatment of her now was businesslike and almost aloof, exactly as she'd always demanded it should be, she thought with irony.

He came and went at Polzion, sometimes being away for several days at a time, and then, just as she was beginning to relax, suddenly reappearing. He was not always alone. Often he was accompanied by other people from the van Guisen-Lyall Corporation, and the dining room became a miniature boardroom. There was never a dull moment, and Morgana knew she had never been more unhappy in her life.

He worked her ferociously, in spite of her lack of secretarial expertise. He demanded high standards and he accepted no excuses. But Morgana could not complain that he was singling her out for special treatment. The secretaries who sometimes came down from the London office to take the minutes at important meetings complained that he was just the same, if not worse, when he was in London. Sometimes at night, Morgana was so tired she was glad just to fall into bed, there to close her eyes and try to stop thinking. Not that she was always successful.

She wished she could hate him, especially in the early days when she was struggling to master the dictating machine he'd had installed in the office, and he bent impatiently over her to make some minor adjustment, his sleeve brushing her shoulder. A silent scream had risen in her throat as she'd forced herself not to flinch away from his touch. Paul Crosbie had been in the room and it had been important not to reveal in his presence any word or gesture which could betray that she and Lyall had ever had more than a working relationship.

In a way, although she had cursed it, the dictating machine had been a lifesaver. It meant that she and Lyall did not have to be closeted alone together for any length of time. She had never realised just how cramped the office was until she had been forced to share it with him.

But it wasn't simply in working hours that she had to endure being with him. It seemed to her that every time she went to Home Farm with Rob, he was there. And she was forced to admit he was a far more welcome guest to Mr and Mrs Donleven than she was.

At least he no longer made advances to her, and she wished she could feel grateful to Elaine for diverting his attention so completely. They were practically inseparable, she realised miserably.

And Rob's attitude created an extra difficulty. Now that he and Morgana were engaged he seemed determined to try and foster a better feeling between Elaine and herself, and was always suggesting plans for cosy little foursomes, which she was running out of excuses to avoid.

Sometimes she wondered in desperation whether it wouldn't be better to have done with the whole charade and tell him the truth—that she was so much in love with Lyall that it was an agony to be in the same room with him, seeing him with Elaine, and imagining them alone together.

She couldn't be quite as blunt as that, she thought drearily, but she would have to say something sooner or later. Rob was pressing her to allow him to buy her a ring, but she knew now that it would be impossible for her to marry him. She had been mad to think she could ever make such a relationship work, she told herself. Rob was too kind, and she was too fond of him, to cheat him with a dishonest marriage. A dishonest engagement was quite bad enough, and there was no way she could go on using him until her contract with Lyall was legally ended. She might have originally intended to do so, and more, but she was now convinced that she would be making a terrible and a cruel mistake if she persisted.

She would have to hurt him, she thought sadly, but

that had been inevitable from the start.

Perhaps if Lyall became engaged to Elaine then he would release her from the contract. Then she could do what she had always planned, and go away from here and make a new life for herself. But it was a prospect which no longer held any appeal for her at all, although it would be better than hanging around and watching Elaine marry Lyall.

She'd not the slightest doubt that was what Elaine intended to do. Jimmy Templeton had gone back to his regiment very downcast. He had escaped from the crash with minor bruises, it was true, but Elaine hadn't even bothered to ring his home and ask how he was. All her attention was focussed unwaveringly on Lyall. She wanted him, as she never failed to make clear, but whether or not she loved him was a different matter.

Perhaps that was as much as Lyall wanted, Morgana thought wearily. If his wife was at home in the kind of world he frequented, and satisfied him in bed, then he could probably do without love.

She groaned inwardly, and thought, 'I've got to stop thinking like this. It's no use.'

Her bedroom in the flat was finished, and even the paintwork was dry, so she could usefully occupy herself in transferring some of her personal possessions up there, she told herself resolutely. There was nothing like running up and downstairs with armfuls of books and clothes to stop you feeling sorry for yourself, or at least give you a genuine reason for self-pity.

The last thing she expected when she arrived breathlessly with her first load was to find Lyall there, looking round him critically.

She uttered a startled, 'Oh!' and the insecure pile of belongings in her arms began to slide towards the floor.

He muttered something under his breath and caught them skilfully.

'Isn't this rather early to be moving in?' he asked sarcastically. 'Most people wait for the furniture.'

She could hardly say baldly, 'I needed something to do that would stop me thinking about you.'

Instead she shrugged. 'Christmas in the hotel business is usually a busy time. Perhaps when the furniture is up here, I won't have time to move my things.'

'Busy?' His brows lifted. 'The place isn't exactly full. Or are you expecting a last-minute influx?'

'It could happen.' She deposited what she was holding in a corner and turned back to him. 'Thank you. I'll take those things.'

'I shan't contaminate them,' he said drily, relinquishing them to her. He glanced at them as he did so, and Morgana saw his expression change. He asked quite sharply, 'Where the hell did you get this?'

She looked down in surprise to see what had attracted his attention. 'I don't really know what it is. I suppose it's a writing case. It was in my grandmother's trunk, but it's locked and I have no key.'

'You could have broken it open,' he said. 'I imagine one of Elsa's kitchen knives would have managed that without too much difficulty.'

'I expect it would,' she agreed. 'If I was sufficiently interested, that is—which I'm not.'

'You surprise me,' he said. 'I thought you were fascinated by your grandmother and her romantic story, Morgan le Fay.'

'Not so fascinated that I'd want to break open her things,' she said shortly.

'Perhaps you should be.'

She looked up frowning. 'Anyone would think you knew what was in here.'

'I think I do,' he said. 'I'll be very surprised if it isn't stuffed with love letters.'

Morgana stared at him. 'You mean from my grandfather.'

'No,' he said quietly. 'From mine.'

There was a silence and then she exclaimed furiously, 'Of all the lousy insinuations! Are you saying that my grandmother—*my grandmother* was having an affair with Mark Pentreath?'

'I doubt if it ever went as far as that,' he said. 'What I am saying is that they loved each other, and continued to love each other and to write to each other until the day they died. It's not just guesswork, Morgana. My grandfather had an identical case to that, full of her letters to him.'

Morgana swallowed. She said slowly, 'You said once that our grandfathers had quarrelled over a woman. I couldn't believe it—but was it her that you meant?'

'Yes, it was her.' His tone was almost reflective. 'Mark saw her first, you see, long before that damned pageant, but he didn't propose at once, because he had very little money and even fewer prospects, and those things mattered then. So he went off to the States to try and make some kind of fortune, and while he was away your grandmother was persuaded to dress up as Morgan le Fay, and your grandfather fell in love with her. He wasn't exactly loaded with money either—the Pentreaths were already feeling the pinch—but he did have Polzion, and that counted for a lot in those days. All he had to do was bide his time and convince her that Mark wasn't coming back, which he managed eventually, helped along by some none too subtle pressure from her family, who thought he was a much better catch than poor old Mark.'

Morgana said shakily, 'But she must have found out in the end.'

'Of course she found out, but by that time she was married. Mark arrived at Polzion, and there was a terrible scene. He tried to persuade her to go away with him, and she agreed.'

'But she didn't go.'

'No, she didn't—your grandfather made sure of that. He said that if she left with Mark he would follow them. Wherever they went, he would be just behind them, and he would never in any circumstances divorce her. He would make sure, he said, that they never had the chance to settle down or lead a decent normal life.'

Morgana gasped. 'But he couldn't have done!'

'Couldn't he?' His eyes were fixed on her face. 'You knew him, Morgana. Was he capable of conduct like that?'

Her mind flew back over the years, saw the harsh old

face, with its lines of pride and bitterness, remembered the terrifying rages.

She bit her lip. 'Yes, he was capable,' she said in a low voice. 'But why? What satisfaction could it have given him?'

'The satisfaction of his vanity, I think,' said Lyall. 'It didn't suit his book to have the girl he'd chosen in spite of herself make an alternative decision. Mrs Pentreath of Polzion was not going to be allowed to walk out on her husband. He'd put his seal on her, and there it was going to stay through hell and high water. And I imagine after Mark went back to the States, there was plenty of hell.'

Morgana shuddered. 'Oh God, yes. I wonder how many times my grandfather punished her for daring to prefer another man during their life together. Oh, not physically—I'm sure he never actually hit her—but there was always so much anger inside him. I could sense that even as a small child—and I was frightened of him—the way he looked at me sometimes. I realise now it must have been because I looked like her. I always thought it was grief that made him shut all her things away like that, but I suppose it was guilt.' She looked down at the writing case. 'Perhaps he was afraid that he'd find something like this—or did he know about the letters?'

'It's difficult to believe they could have kept the correspondence going for all that time without arousing his suspicions.'

'What about Mark's wife—your grandmother?'

'She died when my father was a small child,' he said quietly. 'I don't think they had a very happy life together. He could never regard his home, his life in the States as anything more than second best, and he brought my father up to have the same sense of grievance. It wasn't a healthy atmosphere for a boy to grow up in, and it left its mark in adult life.' He paused, frowning. 'You see, my mother had been engaged before, and my father couldn't get it out of his head that she was still in love with her ex-fiancé—and that she'd only married him on the rebound. I don't think it was true for a moment. Mother told me many times that she and Arnold had been pushed together by their families long before they were ready for any kind of relationship. It was only much later, when she was a widow, that they came together again, and realised what they had going for them. It was a good marriage, they were very happy, which was one of the reasons I decided to take Arnold's name when he asked me to. Being a Pentreath didn't seem to be the best fate I could choose,' he added with a twist of his mouth.

'No,' she said unhappily, thinking of her father and the way he had turned Giles Pentreath summarily from the house. They had been equally obsessed in their own ways, she thought—Giles with his wrongs, and Martin with his refusal to face reality, his pretence that the skeleton in the family closet could just disappear. She said slowly, 'I'm sorry Mark could never come back here.'

'He was sorry too.' Lyall's voice was wry. 'He tried, of course, when your grandmother became ill, but you know how that ended, I'm sure. Eventually, I think, his love for your grandmother and his passion for Polzion became inextricably confused in his mind. He equated one with the other. He'd lost his love, and his home, and I think there came a time when he wouldn't have been able to say with any sureness which was the hardest to bear. He was always a vagrant in a way—rootless—and my father was very much the same, although he'd never actually lived here.'

'And you?' Morgana thought of the houses she'd heard mentioned—the flat in London, the apartment in New York.

'Perhaps that's something I've inherited. I get satisfaction that Polzion belongs to me because there seems a kind of justice in it, but I haven't got an obsession to live here permanently. People are more important than places. If you have the right person at your side, then the surroundings melt into insignificance.' He smiled sardonically. 'But I wouldn't expect you to go along with that. You're as firmly rooted here as the bracken on the moor. You wouldn't transplant too easily. Is that Donleven's attraction—that he'll allow you to stay here, clinging on to the past?'

She was gasping in angry astonishment at the unexpectedness of the attack. For a few moments she had never felt so close to him; now they were miles apart again.

'That's none of your business. I won't discuss my feelings for Rob with you.'

'I wouldn't want to hear about them,' he said derisively. 'Not that there'd be very much to discuss—it isn't a very ardent affair.' Before she could back away, he reached out suddenly and took her bare left hand in his. 'Haven't you warned him, Morgan le Fay, that he needs to put his seal on you in this way, if no other?'

'That's not true,' she said defiantly. 'I don't need a ring to prove how . . .'

'I wasn't only talking about a ring,' he said, and pulled her towards him. His mouth seared hers, blocking off the cry of protest rising in her throat. Then her lips parted helplessly, and she clung to him, glorying in her submission at his storm of kisses raged over her face and throat. His hands travelled down her body, moulding her against him, making her urgently aware of his mounting desire. She flattened her hands against his chest, feeling the racing of his heart under her palms. When he released her, his face was feverishly flushed and his eyes glittered down at her.

'Tell him it's over,' he said harshly. 'If you don't, then I will.'

'No!' She wrenched herself free and stood facing him, her breasts rising and falling stormily.

'Don't be a fool,' he said. 'You may look like your grandmother, but you don't have to act like her. You don't want Donleven. You want me, and you know it, but you won't admit it. I'm still the enemy, the outsider who's robbed you of your treasure, your home. Well, you can have the bloody thing if it's so vital to your happiness. I'll make it over to you, lock stock and barrel. You get the house, and I get you. Is it a bargain?'

'No,' she repeated, helpless tears filling her eyes. 'How dare you think you can buy me! I—I love Rob.'

'You'd probably love a dog if you had one,' he said cruelly. 'Don't confuse whatever lukewarm attachment you may have to Donleven with what you feel for me.

They don't occupy the same universe. I've seen you with him, remember?'

'And I've seen you with Elaine.' Her voice shook. 'What part of your universe does she fill? If you want me to admit that you turn me on, then I do. I confess it all—not that there was ever much room for doubt; you made sure of that. But I'm not proud of it, and unlike you, Lyall, I want other things as well as passion—things like respect and affection, that you wouldn't understand. I couldn't be what you want. I'd end up despising myself. It just wouldn't be worth it,' she ended chokingly.

'There'd be compensations.' His eyes lingered disturbingly on her mouth. 'I'd make it worth it, Morgana.'

'You couldn't.' She was close to tears. 'We want different things. We don't even speak the same language.'

His face hardened. 'You're really going to do it, aren't you?' he said. 'You're going to emulate your grandmother, and let the man you want walk out of your life. You're as big a coward as she was.'

'How dare you say that?' she gasped.

'Oh, I dare,' he shrugged. 'It isn't part of the story as I heard it, but something I managed to work out for myself. She should have gone with him. She should have called her husband's bluff and damned all the social conventions of her day to hell. But she was plain scared, and she let two lives be ruined because of that fear. And that's not romantic, Morgan le Fay—it's pitiful. But I'm not Mark Pentreath. I'm not going to hang about in the background, eating my heart out while you enliven the dullness of your life with fantasies about what might have been. Be a coward, Morgana, but you'll be one alone.'

'I want to be alone,' she said raggedly. 'Any sort of loneliness would be better than the misery of being with you. I wouldn't crawl to you if I were dying!'

She turned and ran out of the room, and down the stairs, not daring to look back, but with the memory of the bitterness of his face etched indelibly on her mind.

CHAPTER ELEVEN

MORGANA folded the last letter and put it back in the case. She looked across the table at her mother, who was still deeply absorbed in reading, and gave a little sigh.

Elizabeth put her own letter down and shook her head. 'What a sad and unnecessary waste of two lives,' she said gravely. 'And you say Lyall has a similar collection from your grandmother.'

'So he says.' Morgana paused. 'Did you never have any idea?'

'None.' Mrs Pentreath gave a small, wintry smile. 'This was just one more thing your father chose to keep me in the dark about. I wish he felt he could have trusted me.'

'Oh, love, it wasn't that, I'm sure.' Morgana put out a hand and squeezed her mother's arm. 'He just didn't want you to worry about things.'

'And that, of course, was the greatest worry of all,' her mother said quietly. She sat in silence for a few moments, her eyes brooding as if she was recalling memories that were not totally pleasing to her.

Morgana touched the split leather. 'Just before we cut it open, I found I was hoping it would be recipes—or knitting patterns. I really didn't want it to be true.'

'Why not, darling?' Mrs Pentreath's eyes searched her daughter's face anxiously. 'It's ancient history now. No one can be hurt by it today.'

'I think it's touched all of us in different ways,' Morgana said. She gave a little sharp laugh. 'At least, I'll never believe in romance again.'

'That sounds odd coming from a girl who's engaged to be married,' Elizabeth said drily. 'What do you want to do with these lettters? Keep them?'

Morgana shrugged. 'As you say, it's ancient history.' She gathered up a handful of the letters and walking across to the range, dumped them on the burning coke, where they shrivelled and turned brown before bursting into flame.

'Rather drastic,' Mrs Pentreath observed mildly. 'They were part of the family archives, after all.'

'What family archives?' Morgana's tone was wry. 'Let's face it, love, the Pentreaths are over and done with. Polzion will be run as a conference and holiday centre in the New Year, and Lyall has no intention of either living here or using the name. So—*sic transit gloria* Pentreath.'

'Don't you mind?'

'There's very little point in minding. We haven't been such an admirable family that we deserve any kind of memorial. We've run the gamut from wrecking and smuggling to sheer bloody-mindedness, after all. Perhaps it's just as well we're just going to fade away.'

'But I thought it meant a lot to you. At times I was afraid it meant too much.'

'Perhaps it did once,' Morgana said in a low voice. 'But it's no longer mine to care about. And besides . . .' She stopped. She'd been about to say that people mattered more than places, but remembered just in time whom she was quoting. She said, 'And besides, I'll be leaving here soon.'

'You mean—to be married?' Mrs Pentreath was startled.

'No, that isn't what I meant.' Morgana sat down again at the table, clasping her hands lightly together on the scrubbed surface. 'I'm going to get a job away from here.'

'But what about Lyall?'

Morgana shrugged. 'I don't think he'll make any difficulties. It's—it's amused him to make me dance to his piping for a while, that's all.'

'Is it?' Elizabeth asked very gently. She hesitated. 'Does he—is he serious about Elaine Donleven?'

'I don't know.' Morgana forced a smile. 'But it makes no difference, because he certainly isn't serious about me.'

'Oh, my dear! And yet there were times when he looked at you, and I thought . . .'

Morgana shook her head. 'Simple old-fashioned lust, Mother, not anything that mattered.' She saw her mother's anxious expression and added, 'And no, I didn't succumb to it, in spite of considerable temptation.' She rose. 'I'd started taking some of my things up to the flat. I'd better get back to it. It will be nice to have a place of our own again.'

'Why, yes.' Mrs Pentreath didn't sound too certain.

Morgana grinned at her affectionately. 'We shall be allowed visitors,' she pointed out. 'It would be a shame to deprive Major Lawson of his after-dinner chats.'

Mrs Pentreath went slightly pink. 'He's very pleasant company,' she said with dignity. 'And please stop looking so—*knowing*. You're as bad as Elsa.'

'What's Elsa been saying?'

'Altogether too much,' Mrs Pentreath returned. 'Sometimes she really goes too far.'

Morgana laughed. 'Perhaps, but it's too late to bring her under control now.'

As she went upstairs, her smile faded as she remembered only too clearly what Elsa had prophesied for her—'Grief and misery, pain and woe.' The burning ache deep inside her bore witness to the accuracy of that.

Wincing, she paused in the gallery, staring at the portrait of Mark Pentreath, now, after so many years, at the side of the woman he had loved. A sigh shook her as her eyes went to the portrait of her grandmother—Morgan le Fay, who had cast her innocent spell, bewitching the wrong man, and suffering for it for the rest of her life.

But at least she had her letters, she thought unhappily as she turned away. Whereas I—I shall have nothing at all.

Morgana was still quiet that evening, sitting beside Rob in the lounge at the Polzion Arms, and eventually he became irritable.

'What in the world's the matter with you? You can't still be brooding over this business with your grandparents? For God's sake, Morgana, it's past and done. I can't imagine why van Guisen had to tell you about it.'

'Presumably because he thought I would want to know the truth at last,' she said.

'It isn't even as if you could change anything,' Rob said unanswerably. 'You worry me, darling, dwelling on the past like this. It's the future you should be concentrating on—our future.' He put his hand over hers. 'When are you going to let me announce our engagement.'

Staring down at the table top, unable to meet his gaze, she said, 'There's no hurry, is there?'

'There certainly hasn't been, but in just over a week it will be Christmas. That's a good time to make it official—an ideal time. My parents are having a party on Christmas Eve. We can make it a double celebration.'

'Are you sure that's how your parents will regard it?'

He stirred uncomfortably. 'They may have been a little—surprised at first, but they're more than reconciled now.'

'Thank you,' she said with irony.

Rob groaned. 'I definitely didn't mean that as it sounded, darling. But they're not the ones who matter anyway. You know how I feel about you. I want to be able to stand up in front of the world and tell it that you belong to me.'

His words made her feel guiltier than ever. She picked up her drink and took a hasty sip. Rob was watching her, not anxiously, but in a puzzled way.

'Well, darling?'

'I need some time to think—I told you that. And Christmas is always a busy time for us at the hotel.'

'Oh, come off it, love.' He sounded sceptical. 'You aren't exactly packed to the doors. And even van Guisen won't expect you to wait on him hand and foot over Christmas.'

'I don't know what his plans are.' Morgana made her voice neutral. 'But I doubt very much whether he intends to spend Christmas at Polzion. He has a family in the States, after all. I'd have thought he'd have wanted to spend the holiday with them.'

Rob grinned. 'Not if Elaine has anything to do with it. I don't exactly welcome the prospect of the great Mr van Guisen as a brother-in-law. He's altogether too much of a go-getter for my taste. He's even had some tame account-ant down to go over our books at the stables, to make sure, I suppose, that we're solvent enough to fulfil his requirements. That's if this riding holiday deal goes through.'

'Don't you think it will?'

Rob shrugged. 'Hard to say. I'm not sure it isn't a takeover bid he has in mind. He and Dad were skirting round a discussion on a possible price for the Home Farm and stables only the other evening.'

She gave him a startled look. 'Your father is thinking of selling the Home Farm? But I thought he loved it.'

'Oh, he does,' Rob nodded. 'But my mother has never been too keen. She would have much preferred him to buy a place in the Home Counties. I wouldn't be at all surprised if he decided to sell out to van Guisen. And it wouldn't make any difference to us, darling. You can't pretend you want to stay on here in the circumstances.'

'No,' she agreed levelly, 'I certainly can't pretend that.'

There was altogether too much pretence in her life, she thought later that night as she lay in bed, trying to sleep, but it would have to end soon. Quite apart from the suspect morality of what she was doing, it was going to be increasingly difficult to keep Rob at arm's length. Tomorrow, she decided, she would seek Lyall out and tell him she was leaving Polzion, and trust that he wouldn't place her mother's future in jeopardy as he'd once threatened.

But when she arrived downstairs it was to find that Lyall had left for London after an early breakfast.

'But he'll be back on Christmas Eve,' Mrs Pentreath told her.

In time for the Donlevens' party, Morgana thought desolately.

She was working on the accounts in the office a few days later when she became aware that someone was watching her, and glancing up she saw Elaine standing in the doorway.

'Oh, hello.' Morgana tried to make her voice welcoming.

'Hello to you.' Elaine strolled forward and perched on the edge of the desk Morgana was working at, dislodging some of the papers. She made no effort to retrieve them as they fluttered to the floor, simply sat there, staring at Morgana, her eyes glittering slightly.

'Mother asked me to come,' she said eventually. 'She's trying to calculate the final numbers for Christmas Eve, and we haven't had a firm reply from you.'

Wouldn't a phone call have done as well? Morgana found herself wondering sceptically.

'I'd hoped very much to come,' she said mendaciously. 'But I'm afraid you'll have to count me out. We've had an unexpected booking for that evening—a family dinner party—ten of them, and I'll be needed here. Please tell your mother how sorry I am.'

'I see.' Elaine looked slightly taken aback. 'Well, no doubt it's all for the best.'

'I'm sure you think so,' Morgana said quietly, and drew the ledger she was working on towards her again.

Elaine smiled. 'I'm not the only one who thinks so. But I told Lyall I was sure that you'd be sensible—that you wouldn't want to play the skeleton at our feast.'

Morgana put down her pen and gave Elaine a steady look. 'And what has Lyall to do with it?'

'Oh, don't let's play games,' the other girl said impatiently. 'You may be able to deceive my poor deluded brother, but you don't fool me and never have. You're in love with Lyall—girlishly and embarrassingly in love.' She gave Morgana a pitying smile. 'And that was something he never intended—although it was wicked of him to lead you on, as he's the first to admit.'

'To admit to whom?' Morgana's heart was beating in sickening thuds. 'To you?'

'Well, I would hardly be here if he hadn't,' Elaine said sharply. 'This isn't a task I relish, believe me. I don't altogether blame you, of course, and I wouldn't even have grudged you a little fling, if you'd been prepared to settle for that. We're all adults, after all, and these things happen. But you're far too much of a little Puritan to gather any rosebuds which happen to be around, aren't you, sweetie?'

'I think I must be.' This was a nightmare, Morgana thought frantically. It had to be.

'In fact the ideal solution to the whole mess might be for you to go away—find a job right away from Cornwall,' Elaine was saying, examining the polish on her immaculate nails. 'And don't worry about that silly contract. I'm sure you'll find Lyall only too happy to release you from your part of it now that we're going to be married. The joke's inevitably worn a little thin for him, and, of course, he never expected you to take him quite so seriously.'

Morgana said very coolly and clearly, 'I think you're disgusting.'

Elaine's eyes flashed for a moment, but she recovered immediately.

'I'm a realist, my dear, and that's what Lyall wants from a woman in the end. Not a head stuffed with romantic fantasies, although your passion over the family feud did amuse him for a while. But now——' she gave a little sigh—'now it's become an embarrassment. And I'm sure you don't want to be an embarrassment.'

Morgana got to her feet 'I'd like you to go now, please.' She was fighting the anger and humiliation inside her, and it was hard to speak calmly when what she wanted to do was scream and drag her nails down the beautiful smiling, patronising face and then, quite probably, be violently sick.

Elaine said gently, 'I think we've had a valuable chat, don't you? I'll tell Rob you won't be at the party. I'm sure you'll be able to think up some story to satisfy him— you're quite a resourceful little thing in many ways. You've just let yourself get slightly out of your depth, that's all. Goodbye, sweetie.'

When she had gone, Morgana sank back into her chair, trembling. She closed her eyes, trying to dispel the images in her mind of Lyall and Elaine together, laughing— laughing about her. She wrapped her arms tightly across her breasts, her breathing deep and agonised.

And the worst of it was she could not run away. She had nowhere to go, and anyway her mother was relying on her for the next few weeks at least. She would have to stay here, and endure Elaine's patronising triumph and Lyall's pity. Oh, God—Lyall's pity.

She put her head down on the desk, and softly and passionately, she began to weep.

In a way, Rob's anger was almost a relief.

'A dinner party?' he stormed. 'Since when has Polzion House started offering that kind of facility?'

'Since I took the booking,' Morgana returned wearily. 'For heaven's sake, Rob, we're trying to run a business here. Elsa's a magnificent cook, as you've always said yourself. If other people think so too, it could become an additional sideline for us.'

'But even so, surely you don't have to be there,' Rob persisted aggressively.

'Of course I do. Part of my job is to prepare the dining room and serve the meal. Or do you imagine Elsa does that as well as the cooking?'

'I hate to think of you waiting at table,' he grumbled. His pleasant face took on a stubborn look. 'If you married me, you wouldn't have to do it.'

'No, I could wait on you instead.' She tried to make her tone light, but didn't quite succeed.

'But I want you to come to our party. I was counting on you being there.'

Morgana took a deep breath. 'Perhaps it's just as well I can't make it, Rob. I—I've been thinking very seriously—about us, and I think it would be wrong to make any official announcement while we're still unsure of our feelings.'

'I'm not the slightest bit unsure. I want to marry you, Morgana, and as soon as possible.'

'And I'm trying to tell you I'm not ready for that kind of commitment.' She bit her lip. 'Perhaps one day, but not yet. I—I've got to get away from here for a while— find a job—maybe discover who I really am.' She tried a little laugh. 'Isn't that what people do these days?'

He was staring at her as if he'd never seen her before. 'You're going away?' he said incredulously. 'Going where?'

'I don't know yet. I should have gone after my father died, but I felt I ought to stay, and find out what the situation was—what Lyall intended.' She made herself look at him, her eyes appealing. 'Please try to understand, Rob. I really do need to get away.'

'Oh, I understand.' His voice was suddenly hoarse. 'I've closed my eyes to a lot of things, and I've tried not to listen either, but it's true—isn't it? You're in love with van Guisen.'

'You don't know what you're saying.'

'Oh, I know. Elaine warned me, but I wouldn't listen. The night old Jimmy crashed his car—there was something going on then, wasn't there? Elaine said there was. She said you looked as if you'd just crawled out of his bed. But I didn't believe her.' He paused, swallowing. 'Is that why you want to get away? Because you're having his child?'

'Oh, God no!' Morgana was horrified. She put her hand on his arm, but he flinched away. 'There's nothing like that—you must believe me.'

'But there's something,' he said heavily. 'Isn't there? Elaine was right. She said you'd make some excuse to delay our engagement. She said all along you had no intention of marrying me—that it was all a pathetic attempt to make van Guisen think you didn't care for him. I told her to shut up. I said that it was all a pack of lies, but it wasn't—was it?'

There was going to be no easy way out after all. She said quietly, 'Not entirely—but Elaine was wrong about one thing. I was serious about marrying you. I thought we could be happy—but later I realised . . .'

'You were going to marry me when you wanted him?' Rob was almost shouting. 'My God, where was that supposed to leave me?'

She shook her head wretchedly. 'I'd already made up my mind I couldn't go through with it. I thought if I went away . . .'

'Oh, you're all consideration,' he broke across her stumbling words. 'How long would you have let me go on waiting and hoping before you stopped answering my letters?'

'I don't know.' Morgana winced as if she had been struck. 'There's nothing I can say in my defence, Rob, but it might be some slight consolation to you to know that I'm more miserable now than I've ever been in my life.'

'It's no consolation,' he muttered, lowering his head. 'Oh, God, what a mess!' There was a silence, then he said, 'So what do we do now?'

Morgana shrugged wearily. 'I find a job somewhere as soon as I can.' She hesitated. 'I know it's trite, Rob—but

I'm sorry. I never meant it to happen this way.'

'I don't think I want to hear any more about your intentions. And don't apologise.' He got up defeatedly from the sofa where they'd been sitting. 'God, the last thing I want is your sympathy. I was a fool not to see this coming. Goodbye, Morgana.' He looked at her with a travesty of his usual smile. 'Don't ask me to wish you a happy Christmas.'

Morgana waited until the noise of his car engine had died away and then went upstairs to her room. She couldn't sleep that night, but sleepless nights were something she was going to have to accept, she thought. However badly she might have treated Rob, she was being well punished for it.

She was almost thankful it was Christmas Eve the next day. She needed things to do. She told her mother quietly that she was not seeing Rob again, and Mrs Pentreath, aware of her white face and deeply shadowed eyes, tactfully refrained from asking any questions.

Elsa, however, had no such scruples. ' 'Tesn't the end of the world when all's said and done,' she announced, standing implacably over Morgana while she forced her to drink a cup of creamy coffee and eat some home-made shortbread during a morning break the girl neither wanted nor needed. 'I read that Robert's cards after I 'eard the front door slam last night, and there's the Queen of Diamonds waiting for him—that Templeton maid, I shouldn't wonder. Ships that pass in the night, my lover, and don't you forget it,' she added a little obscurely. 'He's not for you, as I've said all along.'

It was late in the afternoon that Lyall came. Morgana was in the dining room putting the finishing touches to a centre piece she had designed from scarlet candles and ribbon and pieces of holly. The first inkling she had of his presence was when she turned and saw him, leaning against the door frame, watching her. She gave a little startled cry and her hand caught one of the long-stemmed glasses and sent it crashing to the floor.

'Oh, see what you've made me do!' she exclaimed distressfully; and knelt to pick up the pieces.

Lyall swore under his breath and came across the room. 'Leave it,' he said. 'Do you want to cut your hands to pieces? What's the matter with you? You look like hell.'

'I feel like hell,' she said shakily. 'Excuse me, please. I need a dustpan and brush.'

'Not to mention a double brandy,' he said. 'Don't look so stricken. It's only a bloody glass.'

'But it's *your* bloody glass.' Morgana got hurriedly to her feet, terrified that he might be going to put out a hand to help her because she knew she would not be able to bear it, and that the icy core which seemed to have possessed her inmost being might melt. 'You can always stop it out of my wages.'

'I'll ignore that,' he said rather grimly. 'What's all this for, anyway?' He gestured at the table.

'We've had a special dinner booking,' she said very brightly. 'Ten people. Only a small beginning, but tiny acorns and all that. Who knows? Next year we might make the Good Food Guide.'

'I see.' His eyes were fixed on her face. 'And it's the prospect of serving dinner to ten strangers that's making you look like a ghost?'

She avoided his gaze. 'I'm sorry my appearance doesn't meet with your approval,' she said in a low voice. 'But it won't be for very much longer.'

'And what's that supposed to mean?' Lyall frowned. 'I'm not in the mood for cryptic remarks, lady. I've had one hell of a day.'

'Oh, I'm sorry,' she said insincerely. 'But at least you have a nice relaxing evening to look forward to. The Donlevens are quite famous for their parties, I understand. You should enjoy yourself.'

'I was looking forward to this evening,' Lyall said slowly. 'But my anticipation is decreasing by the second. What the hell's got into you?'

'A touch of realism, and not before time too,' she said. 'I'm leaving Polzion, Lyall. How much notice do you require—a month or a week?'

His expression didn't alter, but she knew instinctively that he was suddenly, blazingly angry. He said flatly,

'You're going nowhere.'

'You can't stop me.' Her chin went up defiantly. 'There's no way you can keep me here against my will, and we both know it. It was all a great laugh while it lasted, Lyall, but now it's over, and I'd like to get on with my life.'

'Away from here?' he jeered. 'Cutting the cord at last, Morgana? Take care—you might bleed to death. And what about your ardent lover? Where does he fit into your schemes?'

She bit her lip, stifling the natural reaction to tell him that she and Rob were through. 'That's my problem, not yours.'

He shook his head, still staring at her. 'Your problems are mine.'

'Not any more,' she said. 'From now on, I'm my own responsibility. I'm leaving Polzion because I want to put as many miles as possible between us. It's you I want to get away from.'

His face hardened. 'Still determined on the coward's way out, Morgan le Fay? Why don't you try being honest for once in your life?'

'Oh, you're such an expert on honesty.' Her voice shook. 'But if you want the truth, here it is. I hate and despise you for what you tried to do to me. Oh, you can make me want you—of course you can—and you're probably a wonderful lover, but then you've obviously had a great deal of practice, and I'm not being added to some kind of grubby list . . .'

'I have no list,' he interrupted, his voice icy with fury and his hands reached out as if he was going to take her by the shoulders—perhaps to shake her, perhaps to draw her closer, but whichever it was she didn't want to know, she thought as she stepped backwards out of reach.

She let her voice drip with contempt. 'Of course not. You probably have to programme a computer to keep track of your conquests. But I won't be among them, thank God. I couldn't live with myself if I let it happen.' Her voice cracked suddenly. 'Oh God, why did you ever have to come here? I wish I'd never seen you!'

'The feeling is entirely mutual,' he grated. 'But don't

worry, Morgana, you don't have to leave your beloved Polzion to be rid of me. I'll take myself out of your life, and I'll guarantee to make the situation permanent.'

She watched him turn away from her, striding out of the room and across the hall to the stairs. In the distance, she heard his bedroom door slam.

Moving like an automaton, she swept up the broken glass, and completed the table setting. Then she went to the kitchen and helped with the vegetables, still in a dream where the only reality seemed to be Lyall's face as she'd seen him last, dark with anger, and something more than anger.

'I'll be glad of them sprouts when you've finished mangling them,' Elsa said tartly.

The Bartons when they arrived were a jolly crowd, so clearly disposed to enjoy themselves and praise everything that was put before them that Morgana was forced to bury her own unhappiness and enter into the spirit of their party, at least on the surface. It was past ten o'clock when they drank their final cups of coffee and departed, profuse in their thanks and swearing they would recommend Elsa's cooking to all their friends.

'Only I hope not too many of them, and certainly not all at once,' Mrs Pentreath sighed, sinking into a chair. 'Oh, lord, there's the telephone. Who on earth can it be at this hour?'

Morgana went into the office and lifted the receiver. She gave the hotel number and heard Elaine's voice venomously, 'You little bitch!'

Her immediate impulse was to slam the phone down again, but something in the other girl's voice gave her pause.

She said coldly, 'Did you just ring to call me names, Elaine, or did you want something?'

'I want to talk to Lyall. I don't know what you've said to him, but whatever it is, it won't work.'

'I told him I was leaving,' Morgana said wearily. 'Wasn't that what you wanted me to say?'

'Liar!' Elaine snapped. 'If that were true, then why's Lyall going back to the States?'

'But he isn't,' Morgana exclaimed. 'At least ...' She

paused, recalling only too vividly Lyall's final remark. '*I'll take myself out of your life and I'll guarantee to make the situation permanent.*' Her mouth went suddenly dry. 'What makes you think he's going back to America?'

'He does. Apparently he walked in here tonight, spoke to my father, said he was going back to the States on the first available flight, and that his lawyers would be in touch over the purchase of the house and stables.' Elaine's voice was crackling with temper. 'Well, he's not going to treat me like that and get away with it. Will you get him? I want to speak to him.'

'Just a minute.' Morgana put the receiver down on the desk and went up to Lyall's room. He wasn't there, and the whole place looked oddly deserted. Her breathing quickened nervously as she looked around her. She went over to the newly fitted wardrobe unit and slid back the door. It was empty, and so were the drawers in the dressing chest.

A little sob tore at her throat and she whirled round and ran downstairs again. Her mother was crossing the hall, on the way to the drawing room with a tray of tea.

'Mother,' Morgana's voice was breathless, 'Lyall's gone! His room is empty.'

'Yes, dear,' Mrs Pentreath said placidly. 'He went while we were serving dinner. I presumed you knew. He told me he'd had a word with you.'

Morgana's eyes were enormous in the pallor of her face. 'Yes, he did—but I didn't realise—I didn't know . . .' She broke off, biting her lip. 'Did he say when he'd be back?'

'No, but then he rarely does. He just wished us all well, and left. Why?'

Morgana shook her head. 'It—it doesn't matter. There was a message I should have given him, that's all. I don't suppose it matters.'

I should have told him I loved him, she thought. I should have told him I'd be his on any terms he chose to dictate. And now it's too late.

She said brightly, 'It's been quite a day. I think I'll go

out for a breath of fresh air before I go to bed.'

'Perhaps that's what you need,' Mrs Pentreath said gently.

Morgana went up to her room and changed out of the dark dress she had worn to wait at table, putting on her jeans and a warm sweater, with a hip-length quilted jacket.

It was a crisp night, the clear sky bright with stars, and she turned her collar up round her face with a little shiver as she walked along. She had moved aimlessly at first, and then, almost without knowing it, realised she had turned off the road and was making her way up the rising ground towards the Wishing Stone.

The Stone hadn't moved that night, weeks before, but her wish had been granted just the same. Lyall had gone, just as she'd wanted, and now she had to live with the bitterness of it. And remembering his words, the tone of his voice, she doubted whether he would ever come back. After all, Polzion was only a tiny corner of the empire which he ruled, and could easily be administered from a distance.

She was tired when she reached the dark, implacable bulk of the stone. She had spent most of the day on her feet, and she was glad to lean against the upright for a moment, her eyes closed, getting her breath back.

The stone was cold and rough under her cheek. In a low voice she said, 'I didn't mean what I said before. Please send him back to me. Please!'

She didn't look up at the cross-stone. She didn't dare. Because if it remained still then her heart would break. She took a shuddering breath and turned away, back to the house, and light and sanity, then stifled a scream as she collided with something that was flesh and blood instead of granite.

Lyall said gently, 'That stone's a fraud, Morgan le Fay. I'd trust your own brand of magic in future.'

She said, 'Lyall—oh, Lyall' on a little broken sob, and then she was in his arms, her mouth parting helplessly under the searching devastation of his kiss.

When she could speak again, she whispered, 'But what

are you doing here? I thought you were going back to the States.'

'And so I am,' he said. 'But not until I can take you with me. Oh, I slammed out of Polzion tonight in a high old rage, swearing I'd go away and stay away until you'd learned your lesson, and would admit that you loved me as much as I loved you. But after I'd called in at the Home Farm, and learned a couple of things, I decided to postpone my trip for a while.'

'What did you learn?' she asked shyly, her heart singing.

'That Donleven clearly thought he'd lost a daughter—you—in order to gain a son—me. It occurred to me that if Elaine had managed to convince her own father that I was on the point of proposing to her, she might have spread her net even farther and caught you. And I wondered why you'd been so careful not to tell me that you'd broken off your engagement. It wasn't a lot, but it was enough to make me decide to come back, and force you to listen to me, if need be.'

Morgana bent her head. 'Elaine came to see me. She—she said that you knew I'd fallen in love with you, and this was an embarrassment because all you'd wanted was a quick affair.'

'Presumably before I settled down to a life of bliss with her,' Lyall completed harshly. 'Dear God! And you believed her?'

'I didn't want to,' she said in a low voice. 'But you spent nearly all your time with her—and you were her lover, so what she was saying sounded almost reasonable. She said we were all adults, and she didn't grudge me a little fling.'

'How sweet of her,' he said ironically. 'And how shrewd. She certainly knew your weak points and how to attack them. But let's clear up one small point right away. I am not and never have been Elaine's lover.'

'She didn't say that—but Lyall, I saw you together. The night of Hallowe'en. You went into her room.'

He said slowly, 'My God, so I did. The fuse had blown in her bedside lamp, and I took her the one from my room, but I didn't stay. You must have a lousy opinion of me to imagine I could go from your arms to hers.'

'I thought she was the one you really wanted,' she confessed. 'After all, you'd said that all you wanted was to get me into bed. There was never any hint that you cared for me in any way. You spent all your time with her.'

'And you spent most of yours with her brother,' he said ruefully. 'The reason I accepted her blatant overtures in the first place was to try and find out just what the situation was between you and Rob. I was terrified that you might genuinely be in love with him, although I was ready to swear that you weren't. The way you responded to me convinced me of that, yet you seemed so determined to push me away. The day after Hallowe'en, I intended to get rid of Elaine and then tell you the truth—that I'd been in love with you almost from the first time I saw you, casting your lunatic spell to get rid of me, that I wanted to marry you, and all that contract nonsense was just to keep you near me. And then the bombshell of your engagement blew up in my face, so I went on seeing Elaine, because I wanted to watch you with him, and see if I really had anything to worry about. And what I found, of course, was you sneaking looks at me with Elaine.'

'O—o—h!' Morgana pummelled his chest with mock fury, and laughing, he caught at her wrists.

'Well, do you blame me?' he demanded. 'You gave me some bad moments over Donleven. The fact that you seemed jealous of Elaine was a hopeful sign.'

'I wanted to kill her,' she admitted, smiling now at the memory of it. Then, suddenly remembering, 'Oh, my God! She phoned the house asking for you, and I left her hanging on while I went to look for you.'

'I expect she's hung up by now,' Lyall said unfeelingly. 'Either way, who cares? After what she's tried to do to you, I feel like throttling her with the cord.'

Morgana hesitated. 'Perhaps she was in love with you,' she ventured.

'Elaine is in love with Elaine,' he said rather grimly. 'Don't waste any sleep worrying over her broken heart. She's a very determined lady. She won't have too much difficulty in finding someone else.' His voice altered slightly. 'Her brother is a different matter. You've treated him badly, Morgan le Fay, even if he did ask for it. He was a fool to let you get away with that sham engagement. If he'd really wanted you, he should have dragged you into bed and made sure of you.'

'As you would have done,' she teased.

'As I intend to do,' he said, and kissed her again, his mouth moving sweetly and sensuously over hers. 'We'll be married as soon as I can get a licence, and my mother and Lindsay can fly over for the wedding. They can't wait to meet you.'

'Oh,' Morgana digested this. 'But isn't Lindsay a friend of Elaine's?'

'I don't think so,' he said. 'I mentioned her name once, and Lindsay said, "Who?" I told you, she has a wide circle of acquaintance and a lot of people go to her parties.' He paused. 'Now, do you want to make any more wishes, or shall we go down to the house and tell your mother our news?'

'She'll be so happy,' Morgana said dreamily. 'She liked you from the very first, even when I was trying so hard to hate you.'

'And I like her—but that doesn't change anything, Morgana. I meant what I said. I don't intend to live at Polzion, and I'm not leaving you here either. I want you with me everywhere I go, day and night. I've made Donleven an offer for the Home Farm so that we'll have somewhere to stay when we do come here—but it will be flying visits. Can you accept that? I know how much this place means to you.'

'Ah,' she said, and smiled up at him in the starlight. 'But you don't know yet how much you mean to me. I'll go with you, Lyall, wherever you want to take me.' Her arms slid up round his neck, drawing him down to her with new confidence. 'Just love me, darling. I don't wish for anything else but that.'

'Your wish is granted,' he whispered against her lips, and above them, unnoticed as they kissed, the great stone rocked gently, then was still.

THE LEGEND OF KING ARTHUR

Cornwall, in southwestern England, forms a ragged wedge between the Atlantic Ocean and the English Channel. It has a coastline of unsurpassed wildness, and it is known for its churches, its food, its history... and its legends.

Most famous of all is the legend of Arthur, the story of a wise king said to have established his Round Table of noble knights in Cornwall. Today the ancient Tintagel Castle is commonly known as Arthur's castle, and to those familiar with the legend the sight of it conjures up a vision romantic and exciting....

That vision is of a young man, Arthur, who long ago pulled a sword from a block of stone to prove his right to the throne of England. It is of a wizard, Merlin, who warned his king that Queen Guinevere would fall in love with the noblest knight of the Round Table... a knight, the valiant and amorous Sir Lancelot, who could not banish his passion for fair Guinevere from his mind. And the vision is of Guinevere, ordered burned at the stake for her unfaithfulness. And finally it is of Lancelot cutting loose the bonds of his ladylove, just as the flame was lit, in a blazing flash of his sword.

What readers say about SUPERROMANCE

SUPERROMANCE
SUBSCRIPTION
RESERVATION COUPON

Complete and mail TODAY to

Harlequin Reader Service

In the U.S.A.
1440 South Priest Drive
Tempe, AZ 85281

In Canada
649 Ontario Street
Stratford, Ontario N5A 6W2

Please reserve my subscription to the 2 NEW
SUPERROMANCES published every eight weeks
(12 a year). Every eight weeks I will receive
2 NEW SUPERROMANCES at the low price of
$2.50 each (total— $5). There are no shipping and
handling or any other hidden charges, and I am free
to cancel at any time after taking as many or
as few novels as I wish.

MY PRESENT SUBSCRIPTION NUMBER IS_____

NAME_____
(Please Print)

ADDRESS_____

CITY_____

STATE/PROV._____

ZIP/POSTAL CODE_____

Offer expires April 30, 1982.

Prices subject to change without notice.

BP459